Walking
on Wild Air

Yvonne Marjot

Isle of Mull

YVONNE MARJOT

Copyright ©2020 by Yvonne Marjot
Cover design by Goonwrite.com
All rights reserved

Walking on Wild Air
No part of this book may be used or reproduced in any manner whatsoever without written permission of the author, except for brief quotations used for promotion or in reviews. This is a work of fiction. Names, characters, places and incidents are used fictitiously. Any resemblances to actual persons living or dead, business establishments, events, or locales, are entirely coincidental.

First Ocelot Press Edition 2020

ISBN: 979-8-6529-5042-2

☽ DEDICATION ☾

For Mark:
still here,
in the wind on the hill.

CONTENTS

	Acknowledgments	i
	Prologue: Return	1
1	Arrival	2
2	Home	12
3	The House on the Hill	24
4	The Happiest Day	40
5	Sea and Surf	48
6	The Writer Without Words	59
7	Moonlight and Water	69
8	Maire Fannon	80
9	The Sea Takes	93
10	Whisky and Water	103
11	Equinox	114
12	Narwhal	130
13	Fairy Gold	141
14	A Cat May Look	150

15	Mountain	165
16	Absence and Loss	179
17	Dry as Old Bones	192
18	The Sea Gives	202
19	The Wind on the Hill	213
	Timeline	220
	Glossary of Gaelic & Scots words	222
	About the Author	224
	Also by the Author	225
	The Calgary Chessman sample	226

ACKNOWLEDGMENTS

Thank you to everyone who helped edit and beta read Walking on Wild Air, from my old Authonomy friends, to Crooked Cat / Darkstroke Publishing, and to Ocelot Press.

To Karen, for challenging me to write a romance in six weeks. Though it isn't precisely a romance, and it took much, much longer to wrestle the first draft into shape, I gave it my best shot.

To the lovely man I worked with, many years ago, who told me all about his Sushila: the kindest, sweetest, most wonderful girl in the world. And to all fathers who want the best for their daughters.

And, most of all, to Mark, without whom this book would never have been possible. I miss you so much.

.

PROLOGUE
☽ RETURN ☾

At the summit of a bare hill, on a quiet island in the bleak west of the world, a storm was brewing. Lightning flickered and dark clouds glowered over the hilltop, their rain-heavy bases lit from within by sullen flashes.

A bolt split the sky and the rain sheeted down, half hiding the ground with its jumbled boulders and sparse coating of grasses. For a moment the scene flickered, like a jerky film noir, and then a figure could be seen on the hilltop, curled up in the foetal position, unmoving.

Thunder cracked overhead and the man raised his head, hauling his body wearily after it. He climbed to his feet and pressed them against the ground, as if testing its ability to hold him. On one buttock there was a red mark, where a rock had pressed into his side, but as he stood in the rain the mark bruised and faded, leaving no trace.

He squared his shoulders against the deluge as the clouds roiled overhead. A great shaft of lightning hit the hilltop precisely at his position, limning his figure for an instant in a halo of blue and white. He looked down at his fists, unclenched them and regarded his hands as if seeing them for the first time. He put his head back, staring upward as the rain poured over his face, drew in a deep, shuddering breath, and howled a cry of pure anguish.

1
☽ ARRIVAL ☾

Late afternoon sunlight touched the roofs of the town, skated across the harbour and bounced off the tourists' sunglasses. It did nothing to lift the shadows under the eyes of one waiting passenger.

There was warmth in the sun, and the hills and houses bathed in it, but the air held a chill. April it might be, but in the sharp onshore wind the landscape was only just waking up to an awareness that it was spring. One ferry had already departed, its bulk rounding the little island that stood guard over the harbour entrance. Another manoeuvred alongside, grinding along the quayside as it berthed, its relief crew pushing past the queuing passengers to gather in a knot at the head of the concrete slipway, ready to file aboard as soon as the ramp went down.

Standing in line among the shoppers and tourists was a young woman with a pretty face and slender figure. Taller than average, but not quite model material: her legs not long enough, her posture slightly slumped, black hair halfway down her back, tied simply in a single long plait. Her skin was brown but sallow, a warm shade faded as if by long weeks out of the sun, or following an illness. She was dressed simply in jeans and flowered blouse, with a blue woollen cardigan pulled around her body by defensively folded arms. At her side stood a large tartan suitcase, looking almost mannish next to her slender form, and she wore a small back-pack on her shoulders. No handbag.

Standing as she did, favouring her left leg a little, a twist of discomfort crossed her face—not quite pain, though two deep lines down the middle of her forehead said that pain was not a stranger. The cold wind gusted in again across the harbour and she shifted from foot to foot, pulling the cardigan closer, then settled again but ended up favouring the same leg.

Sushila glanced down and rested her hand protectively on the handle of the suitcase. For a moment she seemed lost in thought but visibly gathered herself, put her hands in her pockets, and began to take in her surroundings.

A few feet to her right the ferry loomed, dwarfing the figures tending ropes and stanchions. A skinny man in an orange boiler suit grasped a coiled length of rope with a knotted sphere at its end, stepped back and threw up to the foredeck. The rope fell short, missing the grasping fingers of one of the deck crew, and dropped back to the quay side. The young man bent and picked it up, ignoring an amused shout from the deck above, and began to coil it again. A knot of teenage girls giggled and pointed, and one of the tourists ahead of her in the queue took out her camera and aimed it at the man, who was preparing to try again. Sushila turned away, embarrassed on his behalf, not wanting to see if the next throw would be as dismal a failure. Behind her there was a round of applause, presumably indicating that the attempt had been successful.

They'd all been sitting in the ferry terminal a few moments ago, ready to embark. An announcement had been made: there'd been some kind of problem with the passenger gangway, and they were going to have to board via the car deck. Would they please make their way out to the assembly area adjacent to the link span?

Now she was among the crowd waiting for the signal to board. She looked across the lines of queuing cars to her left, full of holidaymakers, to the scattered buildings of the town with an escarpment of hills behind. Commercial traffic waited ahead in its own parking area. Her eye passed across the scene as she turned in a circle and took in the harbour, blue and white with wavelets lifted by the sea breeze, and the islands, off across the sound with the setting sun behind them, waiting for their next delivery of visitors.

Waiting for her.

Sushila shifted her weight again, trying to ease the ache in her leg. She stood on her right for a while, but it was as uncomfortable to hold the left in the air as it was to lean on it. She sighed a little at the pain but put her foot down again, resigned to it. It hadn't improved in the last few years, nor was it likely to. There was no point in complaining about it.

When they were beckoned forward she picked up the handle of her suitcase and trundled it down into the dark cavern of the car deck. People passed her as she made her slow way, but they were all delayed at the base of the internal staircase. Able-bodied folk jostled to make their way up the steep metal stair but Sushila paused, intending to join the queue at the lift doors. There were already a number waiting: elderly ladies with wheeled trolleys full of shopping; an old man in a wheelchair, accompanied by his middle-aged daughter; other adults with heavy cases, unwilling to drag them up the steep stairs. Sushila hesitated, looking at the stairs, but they would not do. She sighed and resigned herself to wait.

"May I take that for you?"

The deep voice at her shoulder made her jump, and she glanced down to see a large hand take hold of her suitcase and hoist it without effort. The hand was attached to an arm clad in a thick, woollen jumper and she looked up, her mouth already open to demur, but saw only the cabled back of it; the stranger had already turned away. He took the steps in vigorous strides, and for a moment she admired the long legs and sturdy work boots. Nice bum.

He disappeared from sight around the turn in the stairwell and she tried to dash after him. After the first few steps she was forced to slow down and took her time over the remainder of the climb, relying on the handrail for an extra boost. At the top of the stairs she emerged into a carpeted area, and spotted her suitcase on a rack against the wall. Settling her back pack next to it she relaxed and began to look around, ready to thank her friendly assistant.

By the time she'd checked out the bar and café, and the observation lounge on the next deck up, they were well out from the harbour and her leg was aching. It was already getting dark outside, and there was probably no point in looking for him out there among the smokers and fresh-air addicts, so she gave up and made her way back down to the main deck. As she sat in the café, sipping a vending-machine coffee, her gaze passed idly over the people going past. Of course it was nearly spring, and visitor numbers were beginning to pick up. She expected to see a lot of strangers but even so, as she searched the faces around her, she didn't see a single one that she knew. Had she really been away so long?

"Sushila Mackenzie. Is it?"

She looked up and met the eyes of the middle-aged woman who'd been waiting at the lift. She was still grasping the handles of her dad's wheelchair, and Sushila realised that her face was vaguely familiar. She groped for a name, but couldn't quite find it.

"Nancy Wilson. I knew your dad. Haven't seen you since you were out of pigtails. Is your dad here with you?"

Sushila took the woman's outstretched hand, and smiled politely at the man in the wheelchair.

"No, no. Just me. Um… Dad died a few weeks ago. I'm here to settle the estate."

"Oh, lovie, I'm sorry to hear that. Give my best to your mum." And the woman moved on, leaving Sushila breathless at the depth of misunderstanding that had just transpired.

At disembarkation she looked again for the man with the cable pullover and long legs, but couldn't spot him. She hadn't seen his face at all, and no-one quite seemed to resemble the mental picture she'd formed. Still, she didn't need his help as she tugged the suitcase down the gangway and over to the bus stance, handing it gratefully to the bus driver to be shoved into storage. She sat in her seat and gazed unseeing out of the dark window as the bus rumbled and lurched its way along the potholed road toward the town.

She focused on her reflection, slightly distorted by the glass. In the dimness it was easy to see her father's features in her face. She stared blindly at and through the reflection, tears hovering at the corner of her eyes, though none fell.

She spent the night at a small Bed & Breakfast, and in the morning took a taxi to the doctor's surgery at the top of the town. In the quiet confines of the housing estate that surrounded the surgery precinct it could have been any small Scottish town, but the mewing of gulls overhead, and the low sound of the fog horn that had haunted her sleep, reminded her that the sea was not far away. The surgery was already doing a brisk business and Sushila waited her turn. She collected her father's keys and asked when the next bus would be passing, but Mary, the receptionist, was having none of it.

"No, lass, we've been waiting for you. Kathy will cover for me. I'll take you up. Poor lamb, we can't leave you to make your way there on your own."

The little car bumped and rattled its way along the road out of town. Looking back, Sushila could see a great swathe of white cloud filling the sound. Beyond it stood the hills of the mainland, a haze of blue and green across the water, and the snowy peaks of distant mountains beyond. They turned a corner and hills hemmed them in. Ahead, rough pastures of bracken and thistle alternated with fields full of fat lambs and a few of the hairy highland cows, some with calves at foot. Beyond the fields the hills stretched away into a purple haze of last year's dried heather, interspersed with the incongruously straight-edged blocks of forestry plantations.

Mary chatted constantly, imparting all the news she thought Sushila might need to hear since her last visit, several years ago. The conversation was a stream of weddings, funerals, locals who'd left and visitors who'd stayed. By the time she got onto the subject of babies she was well away, and needed little response to encourage her. Sushila sat quietly, nodding and murmuring at appropriate places but not really taking it in. Once or twice Mary glanced across at her, looking for something in her face. Looking, but not finding it. She nodded to herself and patted Sushila's hand before resuming her narrative.

It was comforting to listen without having to reply. It made such a contrast with the last few weeks. Mary didn't ask her any sensitive questions, just filled the space with chat. Before long the car turned into a rough track and eased itself across a rusty cattle-grid into a farmyard at the base of a hill. In the fields around the house grazed a herd of black and white cows, looking strangely smooth-coated in contrast to the hairy red Highland cattle.

"There you are, lass." Mary's voice was kind and compassionate. "Will you be wanting me to come in with you?"

"Oh, no. Thank you." Sushila wrestled her case out of the boot and waved goodbye. Mary performed a textbook three-point turn and waved out of the window. The car rattled over the cattle-grid and away down the track, leaving a cloud of yellow dust hanging in the air, and she was alone.

Behind the little house, a great hill rose, cradled in the lap of other hills and sweeping fields. Its crown bore a jumble of rocks lost in bracken and grasses and its flanks provided a foothold for a handful of small homes, mostly let to summer visitors, but one or two still holding a resident family.

***

One of the oldest of the island's denizens stood now near the summit of the hill, at the very edge of a shallow valley incongruously filled with mist despite the dryness of the air and the lack of any cloud in the sky. He was tall and spare, his face weathered, crows' feet showing that he smiled or laughed frequently. He stood with one foot up on a rock and gazed out into the sunlit firmament that lay between him and the little house at the hill's foot. The mist swirled about him and, for a moment, it made him seem airy and insubstantial himself.

He stayed there for a few moments longer, deep in thought. He was accustomed to the feel of the place. Small developments (the coming and going of visitors, the slow daily rotation of the seasons) did not disconcert him, but something had changed. Something he could not put his finger on.

Abruptly, he turned and walked away. The mist swirled for a moment, mimicking the form of his body, then closed over behind him and was still. No-one was there.

9400 B C

The boy lay on the foreshore like a lump of meat, waiting for ravens. He could feel his breath, harsh in his lungs, scraping painfully across vocal cords damaged by the sea water he had swallowed, and his stomach heaved as he vomited convulsively. His furs were heavy, sodden with water that streamed away from him, trickling between the stones and lumps of ice on which he lay.

He could no longer feel his feet. That was a relief—they had screamed pain at him when he first crawled out of the water—but a false one. He knew from experience that it was an early sign of frostbite.

He tried to summon the will to move, but his strength was gone. That was all right. He already knew he was dead.

They had travelled far to the north of their usual fishing grounds. The boy was proud to do so, proud to sit behind his father in the dugout, chosen to share this special expedition.

His first act on leaving the motherhouse had been to enter into the underground realm of the Old Ones. There he was met by kindred become strangers in their animal masks. A stinking sack pulled over his head, he was led down into the pungent darkness, there to undergo an experience he would never willingly discuss with another soul.

He emerged a man in name, with the first tattoo of his people burning on his thigh. He stumbled out of the dun into darkness, disorientated and confused, until a drum beat sounded and the fire leapt up in front of him. His father had come forward then, to lead him into the company of men.

But this journey, this foray onto the sea, was his first act as a man.

His father was dead. There could be no doubt. The two of them had paddled all morning, searching for any sign of their totem beast in the waters between the islands. To see one would bring good luck on the task. To catch one was their most fervent wish: ultimate proof of the gods' approval for this, the newest member of the clan.

They had found their totem. Oh, yes, indeed.

Standing off from a gaggle of weed-girt islands, his father raised himself on his hands, shouted and pointed. The boy looked: beyond the channel between the islands a slender point emerged from the ocean and sank again, between bobbing ice floes. Feverishly, they took their paddles and turned the craft, heading straight into the channel, fed by the rush of the incoming tide. There was a moment of fear as they scraped bottom, and then they were through, floating gently on the waters of a sheltered inlet. Around them, everywhere, the boy could see slick, muscled bodies dancing under the shining surface of the water. This was the very best luck of all.

The father gestured to the boy to remain seated, then carefully stood, balancing himself in the bows. He reached a hand behind him and the boy passed him the bone harpoon, expertly weighted with its straight shaft and attached rope and bladder. The man took aim and threw, the flight of the harpoon perfectly balanced by the line of his body.

The harpoon missed. At the very moment of release, another of the beasts rose under the boat and overturned it. Blazoned on the boy's mind was the sight of his father, arms wheeling, losing his balance and falling, taken by the sea. His furs, and his heavy-boned frame, took him under. He did not come up again.

The boy floundered in the water, grasping for the boat. His hand slid off the upturned hull, pushing it further away. His furs soaked up the water and began to drag him down.

He knew he was dead, but his body refused to accept it. Blindly he struck out at the water with feet and hands, going under again and again as his sight began to darken.

A whoosh beside him heralded a spout of warm salt water that stung his face. One of the great bodies jostled him, rolling him over once, and again. On the third occasion the boy struck back, but the sleek body pulled away and suddenly he felt stones beneath his feet. His strength was just enough to pull himself out on this ice-bound shore, boatless, fatherless and far away from his kin. He lay and waited to die.

After a time, the boy worked his hands under his body and pushed himself up. With a struggle, he hauled himself to his feet and stood, head hanging, an ocean of water streaming from his clothes. He looked out to sea. With a sense of grim satisfaction he saw the upturned hull of the dugout in the middle of the bay, carried away on the ebb, far beyond his reach. Turning to look behind him, he saw a mist pouring down from the hill. Within minutes, it surrounded him, and his view diminished to a few feet. The mist was warm.

The boy screamed as circulation began to return to his feet and fingers. With no more volition than an animal's intent to survive, regardless of circumstances, he began take one slow step after another. Soon, the ground beneath his feet started to rise and he heard a faint, wordless chant on the wind. Shaking the water from his hair, he plodded on..

2
☽ HOME ☾

Pushing open the door, Sushila dragged her case inside and down the hallway to the bedroom. Her dad's bed was coated in dust; in fact, everything seemed to be dust covered. There were plenty of other signs that the house had been untenanted for some time. As usual, Dad had prepared carefully the last time he went away, emptying and cleaning the fridge and freezer, closing all the cupboards and drawers, turning off power at the mains. It was as empty and impersonal as any holiday cottage at the beginning of the season, ready to be turned out of its winter slumber and put back to work.

Sushila stripped the beige candlewick throw off the mattress and took it outside to shake off the dust. She wiped down the windowsill and swept the bedroom and hall, thankful for the hardboard floor that was so much easier to clean than carpets. She remembered running down this hallway, bare feet thundering on the boards, and her dad leaning out of his old armchair to shout something about fairy elephants making less noise. Tears stung her eyes but she brushed them away.

She opened her case and distributed its contents into the chest of drawers, shifting a few items of her father's clothing to the bottom drawer: some old trousers and work shirts, and a few pairs of thick socks. She picked up a folded piece of cloth that had been lying under the socks and shook it out.

Colours flared, complex and gorgeous, and a parade of figures gyrated wildly and incongruously in the tiny, white room. An evocative scent of sandalwood and cinnamon drifted into the air and Sushila caught her breath, denying it, but the smell had already transported her back into the noise and heat of a Sri Lankan market, her hand held tightly in her mother's brown, long-fingered grasp, half deafened by the cries of traders, music from a nearby temple, the honking of car horns, the sound of men and women all around her speaking a language she could almost understand. She held the cloth up and buried her face in it, breathing in the memory of her mother.

For a moment she felt the heat of sun on her hunched shoulders and the touch of a hand on her arm. Wheeling angrily, she shoved the cloth into the bottom drawer and slammed it shut. Biting her lip, she left the room and marched to the kitchen, where she turned on the tap to begin the cleaning process there.

The tap hissed and muttered, but no water emerged. Sushila kicked the kitchen cupboard and turned the tap off, then on again. Still nothing.

Back in the bedroom she opened the case again, pulling out a pair of hikers' walking poles before zipping it shut and pushing it back under the bed. When she reached the doorway she stopped and thought for a moment, then turned back. She crouched down beside the bed and pulled out the case again. The only thing left in it was a small, rectangular wooden box with a square, tightly-fitted wooden lid. She picked up the box and placed it on the windowsill, lifting off the lid to reveal the plastic bag neatly tucked inside. For a moment she looked at the contents, then carefully refitted the lid and wrapped both hands around the box. The wood wasn't polished, but still it gleamed slightly in the dusty beam of sunlight striking through the window. Sushila sighed and let the box rest on the windowsill. She pulled the band from her hair and shook it out, scrubbing her scalp with her fingers as she gazed out of the window.

"It's a lovely day, Dad," she said. "Beautiful spring sunlight and lambs all over the place. You'd have loved it."

Swiftly her fingers remade her plait and snapped the band into place.

Turning away, she walked down the hall and opened the back door, wrapping the walking poles' straps around her wrists as she closed the door behind her. She braced herself and strode across the back paddock, crossing the fence at a weathered stile, and set off up the hill. The eroded gully of a streamlet wandered down the face of the hill, and a long humped ridge running parallel to it marked the line of the house's water supply.

Sushila climbed slowly, eyes fixed on the ground, looking for any sign that the water line had been compromised: seepage from the area around the ridge, or disturbance in the ground. Everything looked fine, except that the stream bed was bone dry. The air was cold and sere, but there'd been no sign of a frost that morning and it was almost April, for heaven's sake. It was weeks past the date that heavy and prolonged frost might reach below ground and crack the pipes, and there was no sign that such an event had occurred over the winter. On the surface, all looked serene and undamaged.

Halfway up the slope she paused and turned, taking a breather as she looked out across the landscape. The broad, rough slopes fell away before her, down to the little house, further diminished by distance, and the yellow track of the road leading away toward the town. Further, in the blue distance, mountains hovered: the great slopes of Scotland's highest peaks, far off on the mainland. The sky was cornflower blue with hardly a threat of cloud, although down in the trough between hills and mountains a hazy hover of white marked the haar still lingering over the water. She coughed, the air dry in her throat, and moistened her lips.

Somewhere off to her left lifted the joyful, liquid notes of a skylark, a sound that her memory associated intimately with the chuckling murmur of the little stream as it fell down the slope at her feet. Today all she could hear as the skylark fell silent was the whisper of a desert-dry wind in her ears, and the distant bleat of a lamb looking for its mother. Far up on the shoulder of the great hill she glimpsed the figure of a shepherd with his dog, a welcome reminder that she wasn't completely alone in the world.

Sushila stood for a long moment, taking in the beloved landscape she had shared with her dad on so many visits. Once, she'd known the name of every one of those distant peaks. She scanned them, fishing for the names in some dark, unused corner of her memory. The only ones she could bring to mind were the twin triangular peaks of Aonach Mòr and Aonach Beag, with their long southward ridge running down towards Loch Lynn, and beyond them the massive, shapeless pile of Ben Nevis. A trick of distance made it look smaller than the Aonachs, but its perfect coat of gleaming snow told the story of its true height.

It was strange to think that at this moment climbers might be making their way up the long slopes towards the summit, slogging through snow with their ice-axes and crampons while she crabbed her way up this parched hillside. A generation ago that would have been Dad, trudging the icy slopes in woollen gloves and long-johns, costumed in the inadequate dress of the nineteen-thirties while researching his most famous novel.

Sushila cleared her throat again, as if about to speak, but no sound emerged. Painfully, she swallowed and scrubbed her eyes. She wondered if there would ever be anyone she could talk to about her father's death, in the way that all those years ago he'd been her rock and support as she cried her eyes out over Mum and Priya. She'd been such a chatterbox as a child, wanting to tell Dad every detail of her day, until he would catch her up in his arms and tickle her into giggles to make her stop talking. Even as he tucked her into bed she would be trying to tell him something, for fear that she would forget before she woke the next morning.

Over the last few weeks she'd talked herself into corners and out again, telling every memory that came to her, in a forlorn attempt to reach the man who'd stood at her back all her life, giving her the courage to move forward. No more. Never any more.

Sushila bowed her head, the curtain of her hair shutting out the great mountains, distant witness to her distress. These days she could hardly bring herself to have a conversation with strangers, let alone speak about anything important. There were so many decisions still to make, and all she wanted to do was to run away and hide. Whatever decisions she came to, she would never be able to have a conversation with her father again. She bit her lip, the pain helping her to centre herself. She'd coped all through his final illness, but now that it was over she was struggling to find the will to go on.

Coming to the island was supposed to give her a respite from the demands of the future. And, of course, she was to meet her father's agent the next day and arrange for the house to be sold. Suddenly, Sushila wanted nothing more than to cancel the meeting, crawl into a quiet corner of the isolated house, and leave the world behind altogether. If only it were that easy.

Turning her back to the view, she caught her breath against a sudden twinge of pain in her left knee. She leaned into the poles, letting them take her weight, and panted against the fear of cramp, but the twinge passed and she began to climb again, carefully, taking her time.

At a rocky outcrop below the crest of the hill she paused. Here the long, snaking hummock had its source, its opening tucked into a hollow just below the rock, gridded to stop rocks and debris from entering the pipe. The pool from which it began was almost dry, its level well below that of the pipe. A slight, constant shuddering in the bottom of the pool marked the slow rise of the spring, at far too low a level to feed the pipe. Sushila sat down and looked at it wearily.

She'd been aware on some level, during those weeks of vigil at the London flat, and then the hospital, that Scottish weather forecasts were mentioning an unprecedented period of cold, dry weather. The stream had run dry before. She remembered a visit here, during another drought, years ago, when she and Dad took the jeep into town to buy up every bottle of water they could find, not knowing when the spring would start to flow again. A few days later, they'd endured a series of cloudbursts, all the rivers of the island leaping into spate and spitting out peat-coloured cascades into the sea. The taps ran brown, and at last clear, and it had all gone back to normal.

Sushila sat down on an exposed rock and pulled off her backpack. She opened her thermos and allowed herself a few sips of tepid water, all that was left of the hot water she'd brought with her on the long train, ferry and bus journey yesterday. She slumped angrily, her head aching. She'd made that long climb for nothing: there was nothing to fix, nothing that could be done but wait for rain. Despite the sea mist there was no sign in the clear blue sky of any rain to come. Now all she could look forward to was the equally long and even more unpleasant scramble back down the hill, with an empty house and empty cupboards to greet her when she got there.

Sushila tipped her head back and looked at the outcrop upside down. Her head swam, but somewhere inside the depths of her mind a memory stirred. Around the other side of this hill, she was sure she remembered seeing another spring. A pretty spot where, as a child, she liked to bring picnics and (illegally) pick the wild orchids that grew only in that one place, the rest of the hill being too heavily grazed by sheep. Maybe that spring still held some water? If it did, she might be able to fill her thermos and have something to drink on the way down.

She pulled herself to her feet and hauled the backpack onto her shoulders. Below her, the haar had thinned and spread. It was already covering the fields between the house and the town, and even the yellow track of the road was softening in the haze. Sushila skirted the outcrop and continued climbing, making her way around the shoulder of the hill, looking for the spring that she thought she remembered.

As she went, she began to see signs of greenness, damp patches in the grass and a scatter of white anemones between the rocks. Then she heard the sound she'd been hoping for: the melodious tinkle of water falling among stones. The little spring emerged from a slight overhang. Mosses dripping with water overhung its small pool, from which a trickle wound its way down the hill. Sushila held her thermos under the drip, allowing it to slowly fill. She cupped her hands to take mouthfuls of the clear, cold liquid before putting away the thermos and picking up her poles again, looking around to get her bearings.

The mist was rising quickly. Its tendrils flowed upwards, obscuring the landscape as they went. Probably this was the last of the sea mist; it would rise until it caught itself on the tops of the peaks, where it might linger or burn away to leave a clear day. She need only wait half an hour or so and it would probably all stream past her, giving her a clear view of the route home.

She shivered as the cold air coiled around her. What was the point in waiting? All she needed to do was retrace her steps around the side of the hill and back down to the house. She could make a pot of tea with the water she'd collected, before heading into town to see if she could buy some more.

She was walking carefully, but the rabbit hole caught her out. Her left foot plunged a few inches deeper than she'd planned and she cried out. The ankle wasn't twisted, but even so the pain in her calf left her gasping. She sank down on the damp turf and hit the palm of her hand against the ground.

"Damn, damn, damn bloody leg."

Gingerly, she pulled herself upright and leaned on the poles again. The first few steps were excruciating, but she'd been there before. Gritting her teeth she forced herself to put one foot in front of the other, until the pain began to ease and become manageable. When she looked up she was surprised. Mist still shrouded her surroundings, but now everything was dripping with moisture. She'd found her way into a shallow valley, leading down into denser mist. Nothing looked familiar, and with the sun obscured she'd lost all sense of direction.

She looked back the way she'd come, but there was nothing to see save more mist and dripping hill slope. The ground under her feet was soft, and scattered bog rush and cottongrass told her it was becoming boggy. She moved a little up the slope and skirted the area, hoping to find her way to higher ground where she could begin to look for landmarks. Her foot hit a soggy patch and twisted slightly, and she moaned as the pain hit her again.

A faint whistle sounded, off in front of her, and she heard a dog bark in response. Sushila remembered the shepherd, up on top of the hill, and shouted. A voice called back in response, and the dog barked again. Suddenly, a black-and-white face emerged from the mist and the dog sniffed at her, backed behind her and began to herd her downhill.

"No, I want to go up." Sushila attempted to reason with the dog, but it wasn't paying attention. The whistle came again and the dog crouched and fixed Sushila with a stern stare: one designed to coerce recalcitrant ewes into line. Sushila giggled. "Okay, I give in."

The curtains of mist eddied as a man strode through them. The dog lay down and panted. Sushila found herself giddy with relief.

"Hello, thank goodness. I got myself turned around in the mist. I'm not sure exactly where I am. And then my leg…"

He grinned at her, broad white teeth in a tanned face. Tall, rangy, comfortable in jeans and work boots, old greyish woollen jersey with sleeves rolled up. Black hair, slightly curly, with a little grey in it. Older than her. But not much older. Sushila flushed under his gaze.

He held out a calloused, long-fingered hand. "Dougie

MacLean." He pronounced it 'Doogie', his voice a warm Scottish burr.

"Sushila Mackenzie," she said, taking it. "Pleased to meet you. I was—"

"No need to worry," he said. "Flo and I will take care of you."

She looked about for another person, but he whistled and the dog bounded to her feet and headed off into the mist. He held out his hand again. "Footing's rough here," he said, "but across the stream the going is easier."

He took one pole from her, and she clung to his arm as he half lifted her over the streamlet and they squished through a boggy patch. When they reached drier ground she released him, but he took her hand and tucked it into his arm, reaching over to relieve her of the other pole as well. She gave in gratefully as a further wave of pain made its way up her leg.

The mist swirled around them as he escorted her over a slight ridge, and into a hollow carved into the side of the hill. In the flat ground at the back of the hollow a stone house apparently emerged from the living rock. Its front portion consisted of a few courses of grey stones carefully built up into walls, the roof of mossy thatch seeming to cover both the stone walls and a part of the cliff itself. The main entrance of the building was a porched doorway whose floor was made of a single large stone almost buried in the turf, smoothed and polished by what must have been generations of feet—or centuries of weathering.

The dog, Flo, was already in the doorway. She barked as Dougie reached out and unlatched the door, then pushed it open with her nose and disappeared within. Dougie stepped back and gestured Sushila to enter. She bent a little. The doorway wasn't low, but broad, and its proportions made her feel as though she might hit her head on the lintel. Inside it was dark and smelled of peat and wood smoke.

She paused on the threshold to let her eyes grow used to the dark, but Dougie pushed past her and opened a shutter, letting light flood in. He moved to the central hearth and stirred the deep, red glow into an orange blaze, swinging round a metal pot hanging from the roof on a long chain and positioning it over the fire. He reached out and took Sushila's hand again, leading her to a battered armchair beside which Flo was now lying. With a sigh of relief she sat on the chair, and he pulled out a hassock and rested her feet on it. She sat up in protest.

"I'll dirty it. Let me take my boots off."

"Rest easy, lass. I'll do it."

With deft fingers he undid her double-knotted laces and eased the boots off her feet. When the left one came free she winced and he checked, looking up into her face, and gently lowered her foot to the stool. He palpated the limb and found nothing of real concern, although she sucked in a breath as a wave of weakness washed over her. When he let go she found the leg was tingling with warmth, and she relaxed back into her seat with a sigh. He watched her face for a moment and nodded, happy with what he saw.

"Rest easy," he said again. "I'll make us some tea."

783 A D

The young woman's heartbeat thudded in her ears as she ran uphill. Clutching her swollen belly with one arm, she struggled to draw breath as she urged herself on. Behind her, screams rang out from the beehive huts surrounding the little chapel.

Unwanted images forced themselves into her mind: the bright sweep of blood as a reiver took off the abbot's head with a single blow. The animal grunt another man made as he forced himself on her sister, his hand over her mouth to silence her screams. The dull thud made by a child's head hitting the side of the great carved cross beside the chapel. And the sense of absence she'd experienced, looking at the crumpled body the raider had thrown aside afterwards.

Dear Heaven, one of them had seen her. She drew her legs up under herself and leapt onward, propelled by fear. There was no real prospect of escape, but she had to try.

She risked another glance behind. The chasing figure was closer. He was taller by several inches than her husband, God rest his soul, and far faster over the rough ground than a heavily pregnant woman. The ground dipped before her feet and she stumbled on a soft patch of soil, falling heavily. The mist swirled down from the mountain.

As it closed around her she collapsed, curled around the cramping pain gripping her abdomen. There was no hope. At any moment he would be on her. She buried her face in the damp turf and waited to die.

She felt his heavy footsteps shaking the ground on which she lay. She heard the panting breaths he took, as close as if he were beside her.

"Odin's Tree," the guttural voice muttered. "I am

blinded." Passing her, all unseen, he stumbled away into the mist.

She held her breath, hardly daring to make a sound, but he did not come back.

For a long time she lay, unmoving, as the rhythmic pains slowed and died away. The child was not to be born yet, then. She waited for the mist to rise, but it thickened about her until her clothing and hair were coated with droplets of dew. Strangely, she felt warm despite being so wet. She shook her hair out of her eyes and stood up.

She gasped and put a hand to her mouth, her muscles tensing, ready to run, but the figure that emerged from the mists was not the northern raider she feared. This was a man she had never seen before. He was tall and lean, without a spare ounce of flesh on him. His hair was hacked short, and he wore a short beard. His skin was covered with blue designs. The whorls and spirals, lines and curves tattooed on his skin deceived her eye. In the swirling skeins of mist, it almost appeared that he was wearing no clothing at all.

She flinched back as the man extended a hand to her, but his movements were slow and unthreatening. He beckoned her to him. For a moment she looked behind herself, to where the sun glowed through the mist and the hill fell away towards the sea. When she looked back at him he shook his head, his face rueful.

"Come, stay with me, child." His voice was deep and rich inside her head. "There is nothing back there for you now."

Trustingly, she put her hand into his and followed him into the mist.

3
☽ THE HOUSE ON THE HILL ☾

Dougie busied himself, moving around the small space with ease, and handed her a battered enamel mug full of very strong tea, and a chipped plate with a piece of incredibly heavy fruit cake. Flo rose to her feet and moved to his side, and he absently caressed her head as she settled again. Seating himself on the old sofa that leaned against one wall he reached into his pocket and pulled out a hip flask.

When he unscrewed the lid the house was filled with the unmistakable aroma of whisky, and Sushila realised that not all the peaty smell she'd sensed on entering was due to the fire. He held it out and she considered it. She supposed that it might not be a good idea to drink alcohol when injured, but in all honesty she knew this pain. It was an old enemy, and she didn't believe she'd done any new or unexpected damage. A few hours of rest, perhaps a day or two of stiffness and pain, and she would be back to normal. She shrugged aside a moment of worry about where she was going to spend that day or two, and smiled her consent.

"Yes, please."

Dougie added a generous tot to both mugs and tucked the hip flask back into his pocket. Leaning forward he tapped his mug against hers.

"*Slàinte*," he said. "Cheers."

"*Slàinte mhath*," she replied.

It was his turn to grin. "I knew as soon as I set eyes on you that you weren't just another visitor," he said, "but at the same time… not entirely from round here?" His eyes flashed, openly taking in her long, dark hair, faded tan, and slender, elegant figure.

For a moment, Sushila was almost outraged—he had practically undressed her with his eyes—but he dropped them again and she relaxed. There was definitely something about him. She ought to be worried about being in a stranger's house, especially as she was in no fit condition to get away, but she couldn't seem to summon up any fear. His diffident, old-fashioned courtesy seemed rather to engender feelings of comfort and safety, and she liked that; and as for the brief moment when he'd seemed to strip away her defences and see all that she hid beneath—she liked that, too.

"My dad was from round here. Donald Mackenzie. He lived in the little house at the base of the hill: the White House, on what's left of the old Mackenzie croft, although the land has gone to pasture the cheese-maker's herd these days. Dad was a writer. He grew up in that house, and so did I."

Dougie nodded. "Mary Mack's grandson," he said. "Her husband was still farming the croft at the age of ninety. Up at the crack of dawn, old Finlay, even then."

Sushila stared at him. He didn't look a day over thirty five. "Dad was fifty-five when he died," she said. "How can you remember his grandparents?"

He shuffled his feet and looked uncomfortable. "People have long memories in these parts," he said, evasively. "Must have heard my old folks talking."

Sushila accepted that, although it had definitely sounded more like his own memory than passing on remarks from his elders. Perhaps it was a Scotticism that had got lost in translation. She looked over at Dougie and he raised his cup again.

"Tell me about your mother," he said.

That piqued her interest. "Did you ever meet her?" she asked.

"I saw her," he replied. "Once or twice. She never

seemed to stay."

"That was Mum all right. She never seemed to stay anywhere. It's a bit of a long story."

Dougie settled himself against the cushions and gestured silently for her to continue.

"I might say that I grew up here, but the reality is that although the White House was one of my anchors in a very uncertain world, I spent most of my childhood far from here.

"Mum was the daughter of a Sri Lankan heiress and a British businessman, back in the days when Sri Lanka was still Ceylon. Very British Raj. But my Nanna, Priya, was a Tamil, and somewhere in the turmoil of the mid-twentieth century she'd lost her family and her land claim, and ended up living in the south-west of the country: a little Hindu woman, lost and alone in a society where the majority Buddhist population looked down on their Tamil kin and treated them like second-class citizens.

"Priya fell in love with a Prince. Well, it's pretty clear he wasn't a prince, but he treated her like royalty. Bought her a house, pretty things, servants: he went away to deal with his business concerns, and her life revolved around the times when he came home to her."

"This is your mum's mum?"

"Yes."

"Sorry, didn't mean to interrupt. Please go on." The formal courtesy of his words was belied by the comfortable way he leaned back into his seat and stretched his long legs out in front of him.

Sushila leaned forward for a moment, pretending to examine her sore leg, but watching him from behind the curtain of her hair. He looked like a man completely at home in his skin, still showing her the reserve due a stranger, but relaxed in his own place and unafraid to show it. She tried to remember the last time she'd felt at home, anywhere, and failed miserably. Anyway, it did no good to dwell on the past. She was here to make some changes and move forward in her life. Wasn't she? She sat back and began to speak again.

"I think she'd been born to a life like that. It didn't seem unusual to her to be looked after; it was just the way things were. But when she found out that he had another woman—an English wife, in an English home, just as she was the pretty little concubine in his Ceylonese paradise—she threw him out with curses and maledictions.

"She never had another good word to say about him, but I don't think he can have been all bad. For a start, she didn't lose her lovely house, although she could no longer afford to have servants and all the pretty things had to be sold off to keep herself alive. And he left her with one precious gem: my mother, Abirany. Even as a child she was known as a beauty, and she only became more exquisite as she grew up."

Sushila shifted on her chair as her calf suddenly cramped. She'd hardly begun to react to the clenching muscle when Dougie sat forward and grasped her injured leg, gently turning the foot forward and stretching out her calf. Sushila tensed, anticipating worse pain, but the cramp eased almost immediately as he rotated her ankle and laid her leg back down on its support. She wasn't entirely sure that the warm, tingling sensation that spread up her leg was due to the aftermath of the cramp.

"Thank you," she said. "That's much better."

He smiled and sat down again. Now she felt a tingling in her stomach as well. It would be very easy to be attracted to this man. She drove down the feeling, refusing to recognise it, and began to speak again.

"From that point Priya raised my mum completely alone. I don't think she had any more contact with the father, or if she did she never spoke of it.

"In her teens, Aby was spotted at the market by some American roué, who followed her home and attempted to talk to her. She knew better, and put him off, but he kept coming back and in the end Priya shut Aby into her room and let him into the guest lounge to put him through his paces.

"Well, to cut a long story short, he was a photographer and he wanted Aby to model for him. Priya wasn't keen, but he promised she could be there throughout, and everything would be tasteful and above board. He also offered money: money that could be made to go a long way in Priya's careful hands. So she let him have his shoot; and Aby's face and hands, and tall, slim, tastefully clothed body, started to make their way into magazines all over the world.

"By the time I came along, Aby was famous. She'd been feted like royalty in America, Europe and Asia, always accompanied by tiny Priya as her eagle-eyed chaperone. But one year at Cannes she met someone new: the Scottish writer everyone was talking about, whose novel had been turned into that year's must-see film. She loved to be seen with him, that perfect white skin and the red hair against her golden loveliness. That was how she described him: the warmth of her skin and his bright hair, contrasting her fall of black silk locks against his perfect, white skin.

"I said to her, 'Mum, Dad's skin is tanned' (I loved to trace the lines in his face) but she said, 'child, I know his skin is pale and perfect. Trust me. I know.'" Sushila stopped talking and looked up, meeting Dougie's eyes as his mouth quirked in a half smile.

"Yeah, now I know what she meant, but I didn't know then. It was just part of the mystery of Mum."

He smiled and held out his hand for her cup, with a question in his eyes.

"Yes, please," she said. "I'd love another. Well, anyway, there I was, sandwiched between the two most beautiful people in the world, and I was the third wheel. The spanner in the works. The reminder that their fairy-tale loving had real-world consequences.

"Sometimes she would go away, and leave me with Dad, and he would be trying to write with me running up and down the hall and complaining that it was too wet to go out.

We'd light fires and toast marshmallows and tell stories, but eventually he'd tire of it all. I'd be hanging out on Main Street while he was in the pub, phoning round the world to find out where Aby was and tell her it was her turn. She would turn up and take me away, into an endless round of planes and countries, hotels and photo shoots, babysitters and friends and anyone she could offload me onto so that she could do what she did best: party, and pose, and perform."

"That sounds quite lonely for you."

"Oh, no, I loved it; don't get me wrong. I adored every minute with my beautiful mother, more like a big sister than a mum, and when she got fed up with the kid she would make a flying visit to Sri Lanka and take me to Nanna.

"By that time Mum had long outgrown the chaperone and Priya was happy enough to be back in her own home, with a servant or two and a little of the faded elegance she'd always seen as her birth right. She would take me up to the market and into the local shrines and temples (she'd been raised Hindu, but that's a very tolerant religion and to be honest I think her neighbours had probably forgotten she'd ever been any different to themselves).

"One day we'd go up the hill into the forests to buy cinnamon straight off the tree. The next it would be down to the harbour to jump and scream in the breakers while Priya marched up and down the beach under her parasol, watching for the moment when assistance would be needed. But it never was. I was a water baby, always completely confident in the water. I knew all its moods, and I was never—almost never— out of my depth."

Sushila's voice faltered, and died. She breathed a sigh and put out her hand for the fresh mug of tea that Dougie pressed into it. Her breathing had thickened and she found herself close to tears. Surreptitiously, she pinched the back of her hand hard enough to drive her fingernails into the flesh. The pain centred her and she got a grip on herself, driving down the tears and the feelings that rose with them.

Dougie watched her gravely, saying nothing. He didn't seem to make any movement, but Flo rose and crossed to Sushila's side, laying her head on her lap. Sushila buried her hands in Flo's ears, stroking them over and over, and Flo bore it patiently while he made his way across to the door and went outside. After a few minutes he came back in and closed it behind him.

"No sign yet that the mist is lifting. I could find my way to your father's house, if you wish to go, but there's no hurry. Stay as long as you like."

Sushila shivered in the cold draught he'd brought in with him. He looked down at her, concerned, then walked into the rear section of the house and came back with a faded plaid blanket, which he wrapped around her shoulders. She grasped it gratefully and snuggled into its warmth. He turned his back to her and lifted the lid from the pot that was hanging over the fire. The slight, savoury smell of which she had hardly been aware deepened as he stirred whatever was in it. Sushila noticed that his jumper, which at first appeared to be simply grey, was made up of a complex pattern of interwoven stitches, all knitted with the natural shades of undyed sheep's wool.

"Your jersey is a lovely pattern," she said. "I've never seen anything quite like it."

He squatted back on his heels and regarded her. "My wife made it," he said.

"Your wife? Is she away from home?" Sushila wasn't sure how to take this. There wasn't any sign of a woman around the place, so far as she could see anyway.

"She died. A long time ago."

"Oh. I'm so sorry."

A silence fell, broken only by Flo flopping down again at Sushila's feet. With a sigh she put a paw over her eyes and apparently fell asleep. Dougie moved away, did something that involved clinking and scraping in the gloom. He handed her a spoon and a chunk of thick bread with a smear of butter on it. Delving into the pot, he half-filled a bowl with its contents and handed it to her. She juggled the bread and spoon with one hand before deciding to dump the bread on the arm of the chair, and never mind the courtesies. Dougie grinned at her, briefly, then turned back to make up a bowl for himself.

Tasting the mix, Sushila discovered it was very hot—she almost burned her mouth, before realising she would have to wait for it to cool—and very tasty. She gestured at him with her spoon, while waving her hand in front of her mouth to cool the mouthful she had already taken.

"It's venison stew," he said. "A fine, local product."

She glanced at him and he laughed. "A fine, locally but not entirely legally acquired, product," he added.

"It's good," she muttered indistinctly, taking a mouthful of bread to soak up the hot stew.

Dougie sat down again, and for a few moments all was silent as they began to eat, but after a while she raised her eyes to him again, and stopped eating.

"I guess it's fair to exchange a story for a meal."

He paused and eyed her, waiting.

"But I'd really like to exchange one story for another. If you're prepared to wait a while to see a return on your investment of food?"

"What story do you want to hear?"

"Tell me what it was like for you, growing up here?"

Hours later she was still there, as the mist outside deepened into dusk. There was no question of her going home yet; her ankle had stiffened and began to ache again, and Dougie wrapped it in a layer of cool moss soaked in the stream outside. She lost all track of time in the pleasant sound of his voice as he entertained her with stories of his childhood. He had her in fits of laughter, telling of the practical jokes he'd played on his older, serious-as-chapel brother, and the times his grandmother beat him with a hazel switch for playing tricks on her. "Not real beatings, you understand. More like tickling. That's what I used to tell her, anyway."

He moved her to tears with his first lambing: the exhaustion of a long night out on the hill, trudging from ewe to ewe, following his father's directions, and the indescribable feeling of having to work his fingers into the ewe's fundament, to deliver a lamb that was in trouble. And after all that the exhausted ewe dying at his feet and leaving him with a tiny, smelly, four-hoofed bundle shoved down his jersey to keep it warm: later sitting by the fireside with it sucking gruel from his fingers while he struggled to stay awake, the two young things falling into sleep at last in one tumbled bundle on the floor.

He'd not had much time for school. "Got beaten by the school master for being useless at school, and beaten by Gran if she caught me staying away." But he studied at the feet of great teachers: brother, grandmother, and the men working the nearby farms. It was from them he learned the skills he would need in the employment he would follow for the rest of his life: shepherding, out in the weather, at one with the wild, cold, windswept world, his only clocks the sun and the seasons.

Sushila watched him as he spoke, pacing the floor at emotional moments, gesticulating with those long-fingered hands that had brought new lives into the world, and seen as many out of it. He told of his first hunt, creeping behind the men through the bracken, wanting to see the deer but not wanting the men to know that he was following. Until the moment the protagonists were all in their places: the hinds cropping the grass, the men frozen at half-crouch, the gun raised to the shoulder, ready to fire.

The young stag raised his head and looked straight at the boy and he'd gasped in wonder, only to see the beast wheel away and crash into the undergrowth. They'd hit him then—not as his grandmother hit the boy, but as men hit other men, a single blow to the face, his brother doing what needed doing. It didn't stop him following, though, as they painstakingly stalked the deer again; this time remembering to freeze in perfect silence as the gun fired and the stag fell.

They let him watch the gralloching, and rubbed his face in the reeking innards. Next hunt they took him with them, and let him learn, and come the day he took his own turn behind the firearm and made his first kill.

"Many a winter we'd have starved without the venison."

She gazed at him through the firelight, seeing in her mind's eye the plaided islanders of Robert Louis Stevenson's imaginings, as ancient and timeless as Homer's warriors or the heroes of the Rigveda. In some ways his life story seemed reminiscent of a past century, full of nostalgic memories, and she fell into a reverie as his words washed over her. At last she stirred, and shook off the cloak of story.

"Dougie, I think I should be going."

He stopped mid-sentence and looked across the fire at her, his face half-shadowed.

"It's been marvellous, and I really appreciate your looking after me and feeding me stew and stories, but I can't take up any more of your time. Could I use your phone to call for a taxi?" She paused at the look on his face.

"I'm sorry, Sushila. I don't have a phone. And there's no road. The only way to this house is by walking. I think it best if you stay until morning."

It was her turn to be embarrassed. "Oh, I'm so sorry. I didn't think. I shouldn't be causing you so much trouble. What kind of person must you think I am?"

"A very nice person," he said solemnly, holding her eyes with his. "With a very sore leg," he added, "which isn't going anywhere until tomorrow, and as you're attached to it…"

"Fair point."

He disappeared into the back of the house again, and emerged with more blankets. When she tried to stand her leg gave way under her, and she needed to lean on him all the way to the outhouse. As she paused at the door, anticipating humiliations to come, he pressed one of her walking poles into her hand and left her to it; and when she emerged, shaky but relieved, Flo was there to guide her back to the house. She settled onto the sofa and put her head down on its scratchy woollen cover, wondering for a hazy moment where he was going to lay his head, but before she could begin to worry about it she fell asleep.

The morning sent a cold stream of grey daylight through the front door and Sushila sat up, blinking, wondering why it was open. She rubbed her eyes with her knuckles and shook herself awake, pulling one of the plaids round her shoulders as she went to the door and looked out. There was still a mist around the cottage, clinging to the trees and long grass, but it seemed thinner. A brighter patch towards the head of the glen seemed to suggest sun somewhere behind the gloom. Her leg felt better, too. Surprisingly so. Usually a setback like yesterday's would leave her aching and stiff for days afterward. Perhaps there was still hope for more healing, and a better return to function than she'd allowed herself to believe.

There was no sign of Dougie in the house and, after a moment's hesitation, Sushila took the opportunity to peek through the central doorway at the other half of the two-room dwelling. This room was darker; the light came in through a single, small window with its shutters thrown back. The nearer walls consisted of courses of large stones, but the back half of the room was built into the curve of the cliff: rock walls topped by the low, thatched roof.

Around the walls were odd items of furniture: a chest of drawers, a small table, a single chair, with three or four items of clothing hanging on its back. Most of the room was occupied by a large wooden bed, piled high with a mixture of blankets, sheepskins and plaids. A large rag rug, very faded in colour, lay on the floor next to the bed. Behind the bedstead was a dark hollow in the wall. It almost gave her the sense that there was a cave in the cliff, and that the house continued into the rock beyond its end wall. She shivered. The room was cool, and there was a draught through the open window. That's all it was. She backed away.

Flo slipped in through the front door and settled herself

near the embers of last night's fire. Sushila held her blanket in one hand, and with the other picked up a stick and stirred the embers, adding a couple of small logs to bring the fire back to life. Dougie shouldered his way back into the room, throwing down an armful of wood onto the pile in the corner. "No time for that," he said roughly. "I need to get you home."

"There's no hurry," Sushila said, smiling up at him. "I'm not expecting the agent until this afternoon."

"No, I need to get you home now. I have… things to do today. Soon. Let's go." He picked up her backpack and slung it over his shoulder, handed her the walking poles and turned away.

Sushila sat and pulled her boots on, trying not to feel hurt. They'd spent such a lovely evening. Okay, it was all her fault for hurting her leg and then following him back to his home, but she'd thought they'd really hit it off together. He seemed to enjoy the evening as much as she did. It had been a healing experience for her, talking about her family to someone who knew nothing about her past. She'd thought he felt much the same. The conversation had flowed easily, and they'd enjoyed one another's company. She was quite sure the feeling was mutual, but now he couldn't wait to be shot of her. Suppressing her disappointment, she pulled the straps of her walking poles over her wrists and headed after him.

She followed in his footsteps as they made their way around the boggy stream and back up the slope of the hill. She was just beginning to feel that the terrain looked familiar when he stopped and offered her his arm.

"I'm okay," she said, waving it off, but he clasped her hand under his arm just as he'd done the night before. She handed over the poles and matched her steps to his as they sidled round the brow of the hill. Strangely, the mist seemed to be thickening again, but the sun was still trying to shine through.

He gave her back the poles when they hit the steep slope

of the hill, and she leaned gratefully on them. Her leg was already aching as she headed down the slope, although definitely not as much as she would have expected after yesterday's pain. As she edged forward she noticed that a trickle of water was running down the gully. Not much of a flow, but enough to show that something had replenished the spring. She wondered if condensation from the overnight mist would be enough to refill it. She didn't think it had rained during the night.

At the base of the hill he helped her over the stile and handed over her pack. "Aren't you coming in? I'd like to at least offer you a cup of tea, now that I have some water."

"Thank you," he said. "It's a kind offer. Perhaps another time?"

She stood and watched him stride back up the hill, the folds of mist sliding over and around him like intangible caresses, the muscles at the back of his thighs visible as he began to climb. "Nice bum," she said to herself, and then, "Wait a minute."

Dougie paused and half turned to look back at her.

"Do you work on the ferry?"

Dougie cocked his head to one side, considering, and grinned back at her. "I used to, a long time ago." He turned and walked away, putting up one hand in farewell. Sushila waved back, until his form wavered and drifted into the mist.

"Seems like everything happened to you 'a long time ago'," she muttered.

By the time she got back to the porch the mist was thinning and rising, the blue sky beginning to burn through. She turned and looked back up the hill as the last of the mist cleared away as if by magic. The hill was empty. There was no-one there.

1774

In the cool autumn air a man and a girl stood on a great boulder, high on the side of the hill, looking out towards the sea. Between the figures and the coast lay a vast gulf of air, filled with moisture and the dancing seeds of dandelions and grasses. The girl gave an enjoyable and entirely unnecessary sneeze, relishing the tickle in her nose.

The man standing silently beside her was tall and spare, body gone to bones and sinew, his blue-stained skin tightly wrapping his long, muscled frame. Every inch of his skin was blue with tattoos, of beasts and vines, clouds and waves, deer, eagle and whale, each filled and surrounded by spirals, lines, circles, curves and angled shapes, in shades of ash and indigo. A mist swirled around him, concealing the fact that he wore nothing else. In his hand he gripped an ash spear with a harpoon tip.

The girl was also naked. Aged about twelve, on the cusp of puberty, she squatted at his feet, staring out towards the sea. She, too, was tattooed, but only on her torso, in places that could be concealed by clothing.

Below her feet the slope tumbled away into green billows of uncut grass, seed-heads bobbing in the wind, and then to verdant pastures, stone walls and low houses with small windows. Threads of blue smoke rose into the air and trembled there.

"Are you sure?"

The girl ignored the man's voice, although it hummed and echoed in her head as much as in her ears. The man sighed silently, and behind him, on the height, a rumble of thunder sounded. She stood.

"The place has been empty long enough. It's time people came back for a while."

"It won't be forever. You know this."

"Forever is a very long time."

"Tell me about it."

The girl gave a short laugh. She stood and stretched herself, humming under her breath. Now, instead of a girl, a woman stood there. Tall and dark, she wore a woollen skirt and jerkin and a waistcoat embroidered with bright flowers. Her feet were bare, and her hair, hanging loose, tumbled over her shoulders. She wore a gold earring, not very good quality: its brassy lustre caught the sun.

She turned and threw her arms around the old man, hugging him tightly.

"Nay, lass," he said, holding her in one strong arm. "I'll still be here."

"I know that. But I need to go into the world for a while. There'll be a man for me, maybe more than one, and people will come here and build their own village, down the way from our house. There's something we need here—I can't work out what it is, but it comes from them. Something we can't make on our own."

"How long?"

"Oh, I don't know. I'm not good about time. Long enough for me to learn everything I need to know. Not long, by your mark, anyway. No more than a few hundred years."

"Take care, daughter. I won't always be able to help you."

"I'm strong enough for most things. And you know I'm not really your daughter."

"You are the child of the spring. We are one, you and I."

"Yes. Yes, that's true. I brought something new, though. Something my mother carried that you didn't already have. We need that again: something to carry forward. I wish I knew what it was."

"I don't have the same sense of need. Perhaps it is because you are female. Or perhaps we are already moving apart. I wish…" The small grumble of thunder came again, accompanying a flicker of white light high in the towering clouds that piled above the hilltop.

She laughed again, a throaty chuckle. "They couldn't handle you. They're going to have enough trouble with me."

She raised a hand above her head in farewell as she skipped down the slope, her bare feet strong and hard on the ground. As she reached the bottom of the hill a door opened in the nearest house and a man stepped out. His face was as clear to the old man, standing motionless on the hill top, as if he stood directly in front of him.

The man glanced at the woman and smiled broadly. Striding forward he caught her into his arms and kissed her. Her giggles echoed off the hill slopes and a buzzard, taking wing, mewed in reply. The old man shook his head. Interesting times were ahead, no doubt, and she'd be less trouble out there than underfoot. This was an old grumble, frequently voiced, and no less satisfying for the fact that she was out of earshot.

He turned away and strode toward the hilltop, the mist flowing around him and taking his shape. Behind, at the base of the hill, the woman was already dragging the man back through the shadowed doorway of his house.

4
☽ THE HAPPIEST DAY ☾

Midday found Sushila scraping at the weeds around the front porch, as the agent's car rumbled across the cattle grid. Sushila jumped up and led the way in, relieved when the woman refused the offer of tea or coffee. The agent took a turn around the property, nodding in appreciation at the cleanness and general state of good repair. It had taken solid work that morning to clear away the last traces of abandonment. Fresh linens made up the bed, cupboards were wiped, and she'd at last begun on the garden. It wouldn't take long to get the place shipshape again, and she'd be free to move on with her life.

A bunch of wildflowers from the verge sat in a jar on her windowsill. Dad's ashes were safely tucked away in the suitcase again. No need for anyone else to know about them. The woman sat at the kitchen table and spread out her papers.

"I have received information from the probate agents in London," she began. "I gather they are putting the bulk of the estate in order, including ownership of the London flat."

"I'm selling it," Sushila interrupted. "I've told them to liquidate the estate. I've got the memories I want; I don't need the possessions."

"So that only leaves the house here on the island."

Sushila nodded, but didn't bother to reply.

"It shouldn't be too hard to sell," the woman went on. "It's in good, tidy condition and there's always a demand for lettable property in holiday destinations. I expect I can have an offer for you within the week."

"I'm not selling."

"I beg your pardon?" The woman was taken aback. "I understood you to say you wished to sell your father's entire portfolio."

"Everything except this house. I'm planning to live here."

The agent looked irritated. She shook herself and straightened the pile of papers in front of her, then plastered a helpful expression back on her face. "Are you sure?" she said. "I understood your main home was away. Sri Lanka, is it?"

"I've decided to live here on the island," Sushila repeated, "at least for the foreseeable future."

"Well, since you're the only beneficiary of probate I don't see that being a problem. I'll contact the probate agents, shall I, in case they decide rent is due to the estate until probate is finalised?"

"That won't be necessary. I'll call them myself. Thank you for your help."

Thank you for nothing, she thought, as the woman backed her car out of the farmyard and headed down the track. Then she remembered she'd been going to ask for a lift into town, so that she could do some food shopping. Perhaps she should have been more friendly.

Grabbing her backpack, she headed down the lane and stuck her thumb out at the main road. Surprisingly, the next thing to come along was the bus, which stopped in the middle of the road and let her scramble on. The driver took her money and told her the return journey would leave from the Post Office at five.

Sushila visited the bank to take out some cash, and bought herself as many tins and packets as she could fit in the pack and a couple of supermarket bags. She added some fresh apples and milk, but decided she could do without luxuries since she would have to carry it all back up the track from the road.

The bus dropped her off and she was halfway up to the

house when she realised she'd forgotten to buy bread.

The driveway was longer than she remembered from the walk down that morning. It was surprising how much difference a few bags of shopping made. Dusk was beginning to settle over the fields as she made it into the yard and dumped her packages by the front door. A small cloud of midges swirled around her as she opened the door, but they hadn't reached the stage of biting yet, and she waved them away from her face and lugged the bags through to the kitchen.

She could feel a warm ache in both her legs, but the injured one had coped well with the day. She'd worried that the weeks of relative inactivity while she nursed her father through his last illness had set her back, but if anything the leg was feeling better than before, better than for a long time. She made a mental promise to do more exercise while she was here.

As she transferred her shopping into the cupboards she heard a soft knock at the front door. She glanced out of the kitchen window and realised the mist was descending again with the fall of evening. For some reason she wasn't surprised to find Dougie at her door.

"Here." He handed her a burlap bag. She peered in to find a fresh, round cottage loaf staring back at her. The warm smell of yeast was still rising from it. Her first impulse was to hug him. For a second she held back, fearing rejection again, but she was far too impulsive to stop herself. He hugged her gently back, and she led him to the kitchen and put on the kettle to make tea.

"I thought you were busy today?"

"I was, but I got it done early. This evening I'm free as a bird."

"Great. In that case you can peel some potatoes."

The meal was good, simple and straightforward, and finished off with fresh warm bread and butter. Sushila was perfectly happy to put aside her worries for another night. Time wasn't going to make her decisions any easier, but they surely couldn't get harder, no matter how long she waited. Dougie washed up and she dried, the simple household task seeming much less of a hassle for being shared. She sent him through to the living room while she made them both coffee.

Flo had made herself at home on the rug in front of the electric heater, seeming to recognise its potential for comfort even though it wasn't switched on, but Dougie had somehow avoided the temptation to sit in the only comfortable armchair. She didn't know what she would have done if she'd found him sitting in Dad's place. It made her realise that she would have to do something about that too, but not tonight.

She placed both coffees on the low table and sat down on the sofa next to him. If he was surprised he didn't show it, but leaned forward and picked up his cup. He sipped it and grimaced, then met Sushila's eyes and smiled. "I don't often get the chance to drink coffee," he said.

"I'm not a great fan of instant myself, but I couldn't really carry a coffee perc up the track from the bus. Still, I hope I didn't make it too strong. Or did you want sugar?"

"It's fine," he said.

"I wasn't expecting to see you again so soon. It's nice, though— I don't want you to think you're not welcome. You are."

"Especially as I brought a bribe." His eyes crinkled as he smiled into hers.

"That did you no harm at all," she admitted.

She wriggled out of her trainers, sat back in the sofa and put her feet up on the table. Not polite behaviour. Mum would definitely not have liked it, and even Dad might have said something. Tough luck. This was her house now, and for Sushila the essence of rebellious freedom was: feet on the table. Dougie said nothing. He was already in stockinged feet, having left his boots on the doorstep. He lifted one foot and indicated it with a sweep of his hand.

"Be my guest," she said, and he raised both feet and laid

them on the table beside hers. Broader and a lot longer. All of a piece with the long legs and the long, dexterous fingers. Sushila suppressed a sudden, wicked thought.

She relaxed back into the cushions and wiggled her toes. "Whose turn is it to tell a story first?" she asked.

"Well, you made dinner. But I brought the bread, so I'm still one up on you. I think that means it's me who gets to ask the first question."

"Bully." She sat up straighter and looked him in the eye. "Hit me with it, Mister MacLean."

"Tell me about the happiest day of your life."

"The…?"

"The happiest day of your life. No cheating. I don't want to hear about the day Father Christmas brought your favourite dolly. A proper adult memory and a good story to go with it."

Dougie was warming to his task, leaning over her and almost rubbing his hands together in anticipation. Sushila sat stunned. She knew exactly what day he meant. There couldn't be any other day. She struggled to get her feelings under control. *Think, woman. Think! There must be some other memory you can fend him off with.* Nothing occurred to her. She sat frozen, and an enormous tear welled up in her eye and dripped onto the couch as she bent forward, curled around the terrible, unbearable pain.

Dougie shifted so that he was facing her, reached forward, and gathered her into his lap. She pressed her face against his chest and sobbed convulsively, hiccoughing into the thick wool of his sweater. He held her firmly, but not tightly, and passed his hand gently over her hair, stroking her into calmness. At last the storm passed, and she levered herself upright, gripping the muscle of his forearm for balance. He wiped the last tears from her eyes with his hand and regarded her solemnly.

"Ready to tell me?"

Pulling out a paper hanky she loudly blew her nose, then caught his eye and he smiled at her. He settled back into the sofa and she shifted to lean against him, gazing out into the room. Lightly, so lightly that she hardly felt it, he dropped a kiss on the top of her head. Somehow, that gave her the strength to speak. "It was ten years ago. I was seventeen."

.

1793

The rain sheeted down steadily as the old woman made her way up the side of the hill. She got herself round onto the lee slope, below the flank of the mountain, and took stock. The hillside around her was dotted with gorse bushes and clumps, their brilliant yellow flowers defying the iron grey of the sky. On every gorse bush, caught up in its bristling thorns, bits of sheep's wool were glistening.

She took a careful look around. It wasn't likely the laird would be up on his own hill, especially in this weather, but there could easily be a shepherd about. Everyone knew the villagers got their wool from gleaning (no-one who lived here could afford the laird's prices) but it didn't do to be caught.

Seeing no-one, she relaxed and reached a hand into the big pocket in the front of her apron. Pulling out a waxed paper packet, she opened it to reveal a wad of tobacco, bit into it and began to chew. She wrapped the rest up in its scrap of paper and, shoving it back down to the bottom of the pocket, began to pull wisps of wool from the nearest gorse bush. A black scrap of rag materialised from the clouds and drifted downwards. It spread its wings, revealing grey and black plumage, and perched on a nearby gorse bush, tilting its head on one side to watch her.

She worked steadily for an hour, quartering the hillside, until her apron was stuffed full with gleaned wool, heavy and sodden. The weight of it forced water through the cloth and it soaked her skirt, running down her legs. The woman shrugged off the discomfort. A bit of rain wouldn't do any harm; it would soon dry. The rain was cool, but this early in the autumn not enough to chill her. She kept a wary eye on the sun: a break in the weather would see her exposed to less friendly eyes than the hooded crow.

Once her apron couldn't hold any more, she crabbed sideways round the slope until she came to a cave set back behind a fall of boulders. From the outside, it looked no more than a rocky part of the hill, but behind the boulders was a dry, sheltered space half filled with a primitive whisky still and some wooden casks. The woman untied her apron and dropped the soggy burden, spreading the bits of wool over the dry floor of the cave. The wool steamed as it gave up its moisture, and outside the sun sent a teasing shaft through the cave opening. The old woman pulled a moth-eaten plaid from a shelf in the cave wall and wrapped it around her shoulders. Her knees creaked as she lowered herself to the floor.

Setting her back against one of the casks she spat out the wad of tobacco and opened another paper packet, from one of her skirt pockets. Inside it was a congealed mass of porridge, which she ate with every evidence of enjoyment, smacking her lips over the last morsel before taking another bite of tobacco. She struggled to her feet and examined the casks. Finding that none were broached, she shrugged and sat down again.

As her body slowly warmed, and the nicotine began to take effect, she smiled a gummy smile and relaxed. From her other skirt pocket she pulled a pair of teasels and began to card the scraps of wool she'd taken from the bushes, laying each piece down on a clean stone beside herself. Outside, it slowly began to rain again. By the time the tobacco had lost its savour, the apron was empty and a huge, fluffy cloud of carded wool lay beside her, free of seeds and dirt and with all its fibres aligned, ready for spinning. She regarded it with satisfaction. It might be enough to make a baby's swaddling clout: a fit gift for the wise woman, in exchange for another pottle of her rheumatism rub.

5
☽ SEA AND SURF ☾

"I met Alan in April, just after the Sri Lankan New Year Festival, almost exactly ten years ago today. I'd pretty much finished with school. The English School on the island still had a place for me, and in theory there were exams to come in May, but I had no intention of sitting them. Mum was away on a series of shoots in America, and Priya was just happy to see more of me.

"I knew Dad wouldn't be happy, but I told myself he was busy writing his next sequel, either in the London flat or up in Scotland, so I didn't need to worry about him. I was in the full flight of teenage rebellion, and there was only one thing on my mind.

"At the time I was totally mad for surfing. I'd get up before dawn to wax my boards, and be out on the water by sun-up. I'd only come in to drink or to wait out the crazy-hot middle of the day. The rest of the time I spent on the sea, catching every wave I could. The whole south-west corner is brilliant for surfing. People come from all over the world for it, and one of those people was Alan. He was an Australian surfer boy: a bleached-blond mop of hair over a tanned body, white with scars from accidents on the board. He was travelling the world with his board and tent, living for surfing, working just enough to feed himself.

"I bumped into him—literally. My board caught him on the shoulder as he was heading out. I didn't even know he was there until I felt his body dragged under the board. He popped up again straight away, bristling with rage and ready to take me down, but for some reason when we looked at each other we both burst out laughing. I wanted to take him back to the house and get Priya to check him out, but he said he was fine. We surfed side by side for the rest of the day, and he paid me the compliment of telling me that he thought I was reasonably good for a beginner. Arrogant swine."

She turned and looked over her shoulder to see if she still held Dougie's attention. He nodded and she turned back and settled into a more comfortable position.

"His shoulder was bruised the next day, so he told me my penance would be to go back to square one and learn to surf properly. Under his eye. It was hard work. He'd been right about my technique. I'd taught myself, and I had a lot of bad habits. I had to learn to balance again, how to stand on the board, how to adjust myself as the wave arrived. He made me stand on the shore and talk through the characteristics of every wave that arrived, to measure the surf with my eyes, to learn the differing characteristics of each beach we visited, and how the prevailing conditions affected the waves. We tore apart the styles of every surfer we watched. We were appallingly righteous. A perfect pair.

"We only had a few weeks together before the monsoon would arrive. By then he'd rocked my world so totally it could have been months. I knew nothing was ever going to be the same again. Come the end of April he was practically living at Priya's house, still camping at the bottom of the slope by the beach, but storing his board side by side with mine. Every day we'd meet at first light, wax our boards, and head down to the sea again. I was having the best time of my life. But I wanted more.

"Eventually, I sucked up enough courage to sneak out in the middle of the night. I sat on the foredunes for what felt like hours, trying to decide what to do, but in the end I got cold and the decision was easy. I crawled into the tent and snuggled up next to him. I don't know what I expected him to do. No, that's a lie. I'd intended to give up my virginity that night, although I was frankly hazy about the details of how it was going to happen. But I put myself in his hands, for better or worse.

"He turned me down flat. Sat up in his sleeping bag and lectured me on throwing away my life and then marched me back up the garden and into the back door. I realised later he'd taken a big risk, because if Priya had found us she would have assumed the worst, and I don't think either of us could have talked her out of that. I knew I should feel relieved, but I was consumed with humiliation and disappointment. I went back to bed and cried myself to sleep, and the next day he packed up his tent and moved around the headland to another beach."

Sushila stopped speaking. Her body still leaned against Dougie's warm chest, but her mind ranged far away, across the sunlit waters of Sri Lanka. The face she saw was not that of the man who sat behind her, and her voice seemed as if it was only speaking inside her skull. She shook her head and came back to herself.

"I spent the morning thinking up all the cutting things I was going to say to him. How dare he turn down the precious gift I was offering him? Anyway, he wasn't that good a surfer. There were plenty more as good as he was. And so on. It was nearly the time for the monsoon to arrive, and the sea had fallen to a flat calm—no good for surfing— and it was hot! I moped around till midday, not knowing what to do with myself, and gradually my bad temper ebbed away. In my heart I knew he was leaving. There's no surfing to be done during the monsoon; the seas are either too dangerous and unpredictable, or waveless under sheets of rain, so all the surfers move on.

"I wiped down his board and slipped it into its carry case. Not a few of my tears added to the salt residue I cleaned away, but by the time he turned up I was calm, and ready to say goodbye. Priya was oblivious; she'd made a wonderful lunch for us all to share. She liked to fuss over him, feeding him up, telling him he needed to look after himself, nagging him to write to his family because she was sure they were worrying about him.

"Alan lapped it up. He was obviously used to being adored by family—he fitted right in with Priya's hero worship; and mine, come to think of it—but when he came that day he confronted me with a challenge that was nothing I'd expected.

"He sat down to eat with the two of us, but he seemed quiet and subdued. He kept looking from Priya to me, as if memorising our faces. At last he told us he had a serious proposition to make. He asked Priya to stand proxy for my mum and dad, since neither of them was there.

"He said he'd never met anyone like me before. That he'd fallen head-over-heels in love with me—I was his soul mate and the person he wanted to spend the rest of his life with. He thought he had nothing to offer a person like me, and he felt the best thing for him to do was to leave. He was going to give up surfing and find some way to make a living, so that in the future he would be able to support me when he asked me to marry him." Sushila laughed bitterly, and half turned to look at her listener's face. "You understand: this wasn't a romantic proposal. He was talking to Priya as much as to me. It was a business proposition."

Dougie nodded, and she went on.

"I'd been holding my tongue, listening to my life being discussed like an employment résumé. I jumped up and shouted that I wasn't a possession to be bartered away, and if I was ever going to get married it would be to someone who actually cared about me and not about money, which frankly is a totally unnecessary and irrelevant commodity. (You can tell I was raised by a family that had enough money, even though we were pretty cavalier in our attitude to it.)

"I ran out into the garden and stood with my fists clenched, fighting back the tears, feeling the sullen weight of the sun on my shoulders. It was unbelievably hot, and the air was still, with that expectant feeling that you get before thunder. Priya and Alan must have talked a bit longer, but after a while I heard the sound of the radio. Priya always listened to music when she went for her afternoon nap.

"Alan came out into the yard. I heard his footsteps, but I wouldn't look up. He put his hands on my shoulders and shook me lightly. 'Sue, listen,' he said. 'Priya's had a great idea. I think it could work, but I need to know you're with me.'

"I lifted my head and eyed him. Heaven knows what I looked like, face swollen with tears, red nose and cheeks, no beauty. He smiled at me and tucked my hair back behind my ears. 'I want to stay here and open a surf school. I know I'm not good enough to be the best in competition, but surfing's my life, and working with you here has made me realise how much I enjoy sharing my skills. Priya says we can use the house as our first base, and teach on the beach here. It's one of the best beginners' beaches in the world. If I stay, will you work with me? It's a fantastic opportunity for me, but you have to want it as well.'

"I kept staring up at him. Stubbornly, I refused to reply. I was determined not to back down until I'd heard something that met my romantic requirements. Above our heads the sky was suddenly split by a bolt of lightning. Thunder rumbled from one side of the sky to the other, and a deluge of water poured down on our heads. Alan bent his head close to mine and said, 'I love you, Sushila Mackenzie. Please say yes.'

"'Yes,' I whispered, and put up my mouth to be kissed.

"The volume of the music suddenly increased as Priya threw open the doors to let in the fresh air. The song on the radio was David Bowie's *Let's Dance*, and the two of us came together, soaked to the skin, and danced in the rain."

Sushila hugged herself and whispered, "That's my ultimate happy moment."

At some point during the soliloquy Dougie had opened his arms and let her go, although she was still leaning back against him. He cleared his throat. "That's a pretty big memory. I'm glad you have someone who cares about you so strongly."

He disentangled himself and stood up, going to the kitchen to run a glass of water. The flow was still patchy, falling reluctantly from the tap. He waited patiently for the glass to fill and swallowed its contents convulsively. The moon was shining through the kitchen window, with only rags of mist still rising from the fields. He stood for a moment, leaning on the sink bench, head lowered as if he was looking at his hands. Then he raised himself, wearily.

"I need to go, lass. This endless dry weather with no sign of rain is hard on the land. And that's hard on me."

"I'm sorry. I always seem to talk too much."

"Nothing to apologise for. The weather's not your fault, and that's what drives me." He turned and looked at her. His face was lined and weary, and the moonlight glinted on the silver notes in his hair. He visibly took a grip on himself before speaking. "I owe you an apology. I took you for a single girl. Not that I'm looking, you understand. But I wouldn't have spoken if I'd thought you were a married woman."

Sushila stared at him. "I'm not."

He looked startled. "Alan?"

"Alan is gone. To paraphrase someone I know, a long time ago."

"I'm sorry to hear that."

"Stop apologising. And anyway—liar! At least, I hope so."

"What do you mean?"

Sushila took a deep breath and squared her shoulders. "I don't think you're really sorry to hear that I'm single, although I appreciate the sentiment. Dougie, you may not be interested in me but I'm interested in you. I'd like us to be friends, but for my part it could be more than friends. There, now I've said it. There's no point in hiding it."

He grinned at her, a flash of white teeth in the dark. "You're very forthright."

"Always have been."

He put up his hands and held her face between them. His fingers were still wet with moisture from the glass, and they left cool droplets on her cheeks. She felt an unexpected feeling in the pit of her stomach: part arousal, part tenderness. Slowly he bent towards her and brushed her lips with his own. The caress was so gentle that she barely felt it. Then he withdrew and turned away.

"I really do have to go. Now. But I will see you again, as soon as I can."

She stood with her back to the kitchen bench, hand pressed to her lips, listening to him walk away. The door banged behind him and she felt again that whisper-touch of his breath on her mouth.

"Dougie MacLean, you are a very interesting man."

1794

In the corner of the house a woman was giving birth. The dim light gave little clue to her age and status, except that she had the full-hipped figure of a mature adult, and her hair was long and dark. At the moment it hung down in limp, sweat-soaked strands, covering her face. She was alone.

Her legs shook as the contraction passed off. She panted a little, putting one hand to the small of her back as she stretched, and using the other to push the damp hair out of her face. Her complexion was clear and unmarked, and her stance straight and tall now that her breathing had temporarily returned to normal. She was not pretty, but would definitely be thought handsome, if not for her eyes. Those were dark wells of chill water, moss-green and iron-grey, and the depths they held were old.

Into the empty room a voice spoke, rich and deep. "If you came in with me, I could help you. It doesn't have to be this hard."

She shook her head, kneading her lower back with both hands.

"No. This child needs to be born fully in the world. If I come to you now he'll be neither fish nor fowl. I want him to be at home in the world. He'll need that."

The other voice was calm. It did not express an opinion; it was interested, however, in her own.

"You think he is not the one, then?"

"If he is the one then he will cross to you without trouble. Being of the world will be no difficulty. It was just so with me." She half-crouched again, clutching with one hand the wattle-and-daub panel that separated the living area from the byre.

A strong contraction rippled across her belly and she gasped, leaning into the pain. Into her mind came a vision of cool water, ripples spreading outward, the calm, easy opening of an imaginary space in her mind that corresponded precisely to the maelstrom opening within her body.

"You can do that," she said without sound. "That actually helps."

She felt a vast sense of approval as the pain of the contraction ebbed.

"You're right, though. I don't think he is the one. A generation or more too early."

"Why now, then? Why not wait until the time is right? After all, you've waited long enough already."

She shuffled around the space, restless, not sure for a moment what she needed. Strangely, the contractions seemed to have stopped. The questions needled her and she snapped, "Because I'm tired of being alone."

"Are you alone?" The voice was curious.

"You know what I mean. I have a head full of memories that aren't my own, and I possess the knowledge of centuries. But I have no-one of my own to hold."

"What of the man?"

"What of him? His love was a brief as a candle's life, burned out long before I was tired of him. He's given me what he had to give."

There was a tense, unsatisfied feeling to the silence. No more words were exchanged, either aloud or in the unspoken way of their usual conversations. The woman gathered her strength. Now. Now it was time.

Spreading her legs wide she bore down, grunting with the effort, pouring all her strength into the movement. She held it for as long as she could, then took respite, panting fast. Her age-old gaze turned inward and she looked deep into her own body, at the great mystery of her womanhood. The urge washed over her again, as inescapable as a flood, and she let herself be carried on it: a tide as old as the first female of her line, a task which her body knew well how to perform.

There was no more room for speech in her mind. The body was in charge, and the task proceeded apace. Far away, at the very edge of her awareness, she felt his love and support: her true partner, down all the ages. Dimly she was aware of a red, wet slither onto the straw under her feet, and a mewling cry. She knelt to see to her newborn: clearing his mouth, stroking his chest, checking all his parts to see that he was healthy. The child sucked in his first real breath and howled in pure outrage.

The woman lifted him to her breast, the cord still dangling between her legs, pulsating gently. The urge came upon her again and she bore down hard, passing the placenta in a single mass. Swiftly, she cut the cord with her knife. With the placenta now defunct, blood loss was minimal, but she staunched the end of the cord with a cloth from the table, as clean as spring water and spells could make it. The child grunted like a wee piglet and fossicked at her chest for the nipple. Patiently she held it for him, until he latched on and began to draw for himself the protective colostrum that his immune system needed.

Now she stood, and turned towards the darkness of the rock wall, as if what lay there could see through the partition. She gestured at the baby, and felt an upwelling of approval in her mind.

She glanced down at the little form, calm now that it was attached to her again.

"This is not the one." The voice filled her mind, but there was no disapproval.

"He is not the one. His grandchild will father the one for whom we wait. It will not be long."

"And for now?

She laid a hand on the tiny head and felt the soft, vulnerable opening of his fontanelle pulsing with the warm blood of his wholly human body.

"For now, he will be who he is. And I will be his mother."

6
☽ THE WRITER WITHOUT WORDS ☾

The morning came in cool and fresh, another dry day with hardly a wisp of cloud in the heavens. Today there was no mist over the sea, and the hills stood out stark against the sky. There was hardly a mention of moisture in the weather forecast. Sushila stood in a queue at the little supermarket and listened to the flow of talk around her. Apparently it had already been the driest winter for sixty years, and it was shaping up to be a record-breaking dry spring.

On her way back up the track with a new supply of food, her backpack weighed down by a five-litre bottle of water, she noticed the dusty road edges and drooping wild flowers. Snowdrops and daffodils had come and gone as usual, but the newly sprouted foliage of bluebells was brown and shrivelled by frost, and the grass was yellowing. Even the mosses that edged the drainage ditches were shrunken and brittle looking. Sushila wondered how long people could manage without rain. Springs must be drying up all over the island, and many farms and isolated houses depended on spring-fed streams for their water supply.

She spent the afternoon wasting some of her precious water scrubbing the floors, but used an alcohol-based spray and a couple of old tea-towels to clean the windows. When every surface was gleaming, and the windows dazzling in the sunshine, she dragged a kitchen chair out through the back door and sat in the yard with a long, cool glass of lemonade, soaking up the sun as it slowly made its way behind the hill. There was no water in the tap (the spring had probably dried up again) and she poured a little water from the plastic bottle to wash in, and used the dirty water to irrigate a lonely and hopeful tulip that was struggling through the dry soil in a planter beside the back door.

As darkness settled over the landscape, a crescent moon brightened into existence above the distant lights of the town. Sushila made her bed, then sat down on it, deep in thought. She'd travelled all the way up here for a reason. It would have been easy enough to phone the solicitor from London and have her sell the house.

After all, it was Dad's home, not hers, for all that it held many good memories for her. Between Dad's money and Mum's she could live wherever she wanted. It wasn't necessary to go anywhere that held memories, but for some reason she'd felt compelled to run back here. If all she wanted was to hide herself away from the world, well, then, here was as good as anywhere, but the truth was that she didn't know what she wanted to do.

She stood and paced the floor, then sat down again and pushed her fists between her knees, rocking forward. At the very least she had to make some kind of decision about Dad's ashes. She knew what he would have wanted. He'd have wanted to be with Mum. Of course that was impossible.

If only he'd told her what to do, or left some indication in his will. She'd been avoiding him for such a long time, for most of the last ten years really, unable to bear the thought of seeing in his face the unwanted sympathy and compassion that he couldn't stop himself from offering. Their occasional exchanges of letters were full of platitudes and gentle good wishes but carefully free of any real information or emotional baggage.

When the call came, and she'd gone home, he wasn't well enough for anything but quiet, undemanding conversations, and gentle, careful care. He'd had a stroke a few months before, but hadn't told her about it. *Bloody independent minded...* She grimaced, recognising herself in the description. *I have to admit, I came by that honestly.*

The second stroke robbed him of all but the most rudimentary speech. She set herself up in his bedroom in the London flat (he'd already been sleeping on a bed in the living room, closer to the facilities) and within weeks he deteriorated further. Finally, she took the decision to admit him to hospital. She made sure he was given all the best care the world could offer, but nothing could halt the slow advance of time. He ebbed quietly away from her, his eyes becoming vague and distant, his hand slipping from hers.

She sat by his bedside and talked and talked, filling the space left empty by his wonderful conversations, his endless lectures, his subtle and clever humour; and all the time she talked he gazed at her, holding her hand, murmuring the only word he had left, "Wait... wait... wait."

Every night she went home and crawled into his bed, pulled his pillow against her face, fought to hold onto her memories of him. And every morning took herself back, feeling the memories slipping away, replacing them with white room and white sheets and white, bloodless face and fingers. When sleep eluded her altogether she compulsively read his novels, working her way through them from earliest to latest, recognising in every line the inspiration he'd taken from her mother, from Scotland and Sri Lanka, from her.

Sushila hit the heels of her hands against her forehead and moaned. Now she was sitting in another white room, more alone than ever, the ashes in their box under the bed no worse a companion than the writer without words; the scintillating conversationalist without speech; the lively, intelligent mind left without the ability to communicate. She wasn't convinced he'd died from any physical cause. The hospital provided a high standard of care, and there was no reason to believe a third stroke was any more likely than the second had been.

"Just one of those things," the registrar had said, in a singularly unmedical way. But it seemed to Sushila that without communication her father had dwindled, shrunk—

given up. Without his writing, and most of all without conversation, he had nothing left to live for.

"Except me," she whispered into the dead air of the dead room. "What am I going to do now?"

Another day came and went, and she was no closer to making any kind of decision. Dumping Dad's ashes outside the house would feel wrong (it was where he lived from time to time, not where his heart was) but she really, really didn't want to carry them round with her forever. He definitely wouldn't have wanted that.

To be fair, he would probably be perfectly happy if she dumped them in the garden and planted a wild rose on top, but Sushila wanted to find a solution that was satisfying to her. This was the last thing she could do for her father, and for once in her life she wanted to get it right.

She decided to set the problem aside again, and packed a batch of fresh scones and a bottle of lemonade into her backpack. She told herself she was just exploring and using the leg, trying to build up strength, but it was no good lying to herself: she was going to look for Dougie.

All right, perhaps she was jumping the gun going in search of him today—it had only been two days since they'd spent the evening together—but Sushila's natural impatience coupled with the sense of being trapped, so different from the feeling of sanctuary that she'd hoped to experience in her father's house, combined to drive her into action. As she grabbed her poles and set off she reminded herself she needed the exercise, and that was true enough.

This time she made sure to take her fully-charged mobile phone. There was no point in taking chances. That characteristic crease wrinkled her forehead as she stared down at the phone's tiny screen. No signal. A common problem here on the island, which had bothered her father not at all. He'd liked the sense of isolation in the tiny cottage up a dirt road, with no phone line and no mobile signal. It was possible to get quite a good signal if you climbed the hill, but the house had never been able to receive calls. That was as good an excuse as any for the fact that Dougie hadn't contacted her again. Although come to think of it, he'd told her he didn't have a phone. Surely these days everybody has a mobile?

The grass on the hillside was crisp and the ground hard. Sushila pushed herself into the climb, and made it up to the springhead in good time. The leg felt fine. All the walking over the last few days must have done some good. She checked her phone and found a full four bars of signal, so took a break and used the opportunity to phone Mary at the surgery. A few moments of explanation were all that was needed; Mary would come to the house the next day with a delivery of bottled water. She seemed only too happy to help.

Sushila hung up and sat for a while, gazing at the spring burbling in the depths of its hollow. It occurred to her that she liked Mary. It had been surprisingly nice to chat to a friend, something she wasn't in the habit of doing. Over the last couple of days her energy levels seemed to have shot up, although they'd fluctuated weirdly during the evening she'd spent with Dougie. The mundane explanation for that was undoubtedly shock from aggravating the injury. Looking for any more complex reason was uncalled for.

A cold finger of wind crossed her shoulder blades and she shivered. *Pull yourself together, woman.* She stood up and got her bearings, then pushed off in the direction she was sure she'd gone the last time she'd looked for the second spring. This time she couldn't locate it. In fact, she couldn't find any of the signs she'd used to track the presence of water in the landscape. The grass continued dry and yellowing, and there were none of the patches of wild flowers she'd remembered seeing. She traversed the entire hilltop, back to her own spring, without seeing any other sign of water.

The second time round she took a wider circle, trying to identify the valley she'd accidentally made her way into, thinking that if she could stumble into it again she would soon find Dougie's house. She did find her way into a shallow valley that fell away from the side of the hill, and she scrambled down its side, expecting to find boggy ground at the bottom, but the little valley was as dry as a bone, filled with scree and a thin coating of rough grass.

Further down, the slope bottomed out, with a rocky wall along one side that was vaguely reminiscent of the area around Dougie's house. There were walls and corners emerging from the dusty ground, no more than a course or two of tumbled stones, the occasional squared-off edge or doorway-sized gap suggesting that she had come across the remains of an abandoned village, but no house, no stream, and definitely no Dougie.

She stood in the middle of the dusty valley and shouted, hoping that Flo would hear her, if not the man himself. In the end she had to admit to herself that she was in completely the wrong place. She must have got turned around in the mist that day and wandered off onto some other hillside altogether. She grumbled her way up the slope to the ridge top and found her way back to her own familiar spring. The water looked lower than ever, and leaning over she could see it bubbling up between the stones at the bottom of the pool.

Sushila ate some scones and washed them down with lemonade. There was clearly going to be no opportunity to share them today. She sat on for a while next to the spring. There was something magical about the slow, steady upwelling of water from the dry land. The spring level had dropped again recently, and the lowest few centimetres of exposed stone was coated with a slime of green algae, now drying rapidly in the parched air. Above it, the mosses, ferns and liverworts that usually overhung the pool were limp and wilted. Whatever reservoir of water remained in the heart of the hill, it was laying very low. If the weather got any drier the spring would stop entirely, and then who knew what would happen even if it did rain.

Behind her shoulder a little wind stirred the long grass and moved gently over the hill. It paused to caress her cheek with the lightest of touches, but died away again in the hot air. A buzzard rose in the sky above her house, lifting itself on one of the thermals that develop near hills on hot still days. She watched it climb higher and higher until it was only a speck in the heavens. That made her realise that it probably wasn't a buzzard; they didn't climb so high. Perhaps this was her first glimpse of a golden eagle. Magic.

1802

The boy dragged another armful of dried kelp across the foreshore and laid it on the smoky pile to burn. The pungent fumes caught in the back of his throat and made him cough. He stood and moved away from the smoke, which streamed inland on the breeze off the loch. He glanced across at his mother.

She stood straight and tall, with the bearing of a woman in her prime, but her skin was beginning to line and her eyes were, well, odd. He didn't like to look into those eyes: they always gave him the feeling he was falling into a deep pool, with no way of knowing what was at the bottom. He turned away and looked where she was looking.

Away up on the hill, figures were trudging downslope, flanked by men on horseback. Behind them, over the ridge, thin lines of smoke were rising into the air, five or six of them, quivering in the summer haze. Behind him, Mother began a sing-song chant in the Gaelic, low and quiet, just at the edge of hearing.

Some of the mounted men wore red coats. Campbells: the laird's men. One, astride a sturdy bay mare, was the factor, unmistakable in his fine tweed jacket.

"Don't look, boy. They'll sense your eyes."

Accustomed to obey, the boy turned his head, but couldn't help but glance out of the corner of his eye. It looked as though all the folk of the village—*cailleachs*, bairns and all—were coming down the hill, herded by the horsemen.

One of the riders turned his horse and moved in their direction.

The woman hissed behind her teeth and spoke out of

the side of her mouth. "Behind me, *a bhalaich*. Head down, stay still and *don't look*."

He ducked behind her skirts and crouched on the shingle, looking out to sea. He could hear the shush of the horse's flanks as it forced its way through the long grass onto the shore. Its hooves clinked on the shingle. The droning song grew a little louder.

The rider must have been standing within yards of them. The boy could see him in his mind's eye: the proud neck of the horse, the sweat-stained coat and muddy boots, even a scorch mark on the trousers. He wore a twist of Campbell tartan round his neck, tucked into the front of his coat.

The man brushed his thigh with his hand, as if he'd heard the boy's thoughts. He stood for a moment, looking out across the water, seeing what he was meant to see: shingle, seaweed, a single curlew. Nothing of any interest. He paid no attention to the woman on the foreshore.

After a long moment, he clucked under his breath and the horse turned away, taking sliding steps across the shingle and then back up the bank on to the hillside. The grey horse and its rider followed the evicted villagers and their escort down towards the road, and the town. The boy glanced up at his mother. Her face was stern, but she let the song die away to a whisper.

"Where are they going, Mam?"

"Away, *a bhobain*. Away to the coasts, to the mainland, to Canada. Who's to say?"

"Why? Why are they going?"

"Because the land is needed for sheep. There's no place for the people in all this wide land." The bottomless green pools of her eyes shone with unshed tears as she led the way back up the hillside. The boy trotted behind her, hardly content with the answer, but unwilling to ask for more.

He got all the explanation that was needed when they reached the village. Not a house was left standing. Doors were kicked in, or torn off their hinges. Thatch had been set alight, and stone walls at least partly pushed over. Two houses were now represented only by a steaming pile of carbonised ash and the tumbled stones that had once weighted down the thatch-netting.

Not a house still stood, bar one. His mother's house on its stone plinth, built into the living rock of the cliff, stood as though nothing had touched it; saved, perhaps, by its distance from the other houses of the settlement. A coil of smoke emerged from the chimney, suggesting that one of the smooring peats had shifted, but the roof was untouched. The woman reached and pulled a thin piece of straw from the door hinge, just below the lintel. She blew it away and opened the door.

Still silent, the boy followed her in. It might come in useful, that song of Mam's. Especially if Mother Morag was making bannocks and he wanted to get himself one without her noticing. A grin flashed across his face, before it dawned on him that Morag would be making no more bannocks, at least not here. The grin disappeared as quickly as it had come, as he realised that there was no more village. No friends. No enemies. No angry mothers, or impatient fathers quick with fists.

There was only his Mam, and himself.

7
☽ MOONLIGHT AND WATER ☾

Mary helped her finish off the scones the next day. She supplied Sushila with enough bottled water to survive a siege, and a pithy lecture on the dangers of drinking untreated water. She also kidnapped her, and took her out to lunch with the ladies from the surgery: Kathy from the office, Morgan and Janet from the Health Visitor team, and Ellie from the dental clinic next door. It was the quiet spot in the day between morning and afternoon surgeries, so Dr Kim put the phone calls through to her office and was holding the fort while downing a few sandwiches and reading over notes for the afternoon's appointments.

They were a noisy, cheerful gang and swept Sushila along with them. By the time they reached the pub and placed their orders she'd already revealed her current mission (Dad's ashes), her plans for Dad's properties (selling the London flat, haven't decided about the island house yet) and her seafood preferences (love mussels, can't stand scallops, won't eat crab if you pay me). She sank down on a wooden bench and sipped her beer, slightly shaken by the ease with which the women had included her in their non-stop round of gossip and complaint.

She discovered that Kathy was recovering from breast cancer, Ellie was waiting for surgery for persistent tonsillitis, and Janet was fighting her ex-husband over the divorce settlement but was of half a mind to tell him where to stick it, if only she didn't need the money to put their son through university. Morgan was the quietest of them all and hadn't volunteered any personal information yet, but Sushila was sure it was only a matter of time.

They all seemed delighted with her suggestion that she might stay on at her father's cottage, and came up with helpful suggestions about where she might find work. Sushila admitted she hadn't really thought about that. It's not as though a failed surf-school and a stint as general factotum in an orphanage are really good preparation for any other kind of work. She supposed there must always be bar and waitressing work, if she could train herself to stand for any length of time, although the leg might not allow for it.

An hour later they parted at the surgery, Mary driving on to drop Sushila at her door before proceeding to her father's house where he was due for a weekly visit, which Mary would combine with feeding him a proper cooked meal and giving the place "the once over." Her comment had the ring of a well-aired complaint. "It's not as if he can really do for himself any more. H does get meals on wheels, but it's not as nice as a proper home-cooked dinner."

Lunch had been a lovely surprise, but by the time Sushila stumbled out of the car and waved Mary off she felt she'd had a surfeit of company. A pleasant lunch with only one or two beers was more than enough for someone who hadn't drunk anything stronger than tea with a dash of whisky for months.

She was no further forward in dealing with the Dad problem. Dougie seemed to have disappeared off the face of the earth. The ladies who lunched were lovely but hadn't provided her with any answers, although their questions certainly gave her food for thought. It began to dawn on her that if she wanted to stay on the island, she needed a reason to stay. It did no good to say 'running away.' One had then to admit 'running away from what?' And if she wasn't going to face up to that question, she needed to come up with some other reason for being here. Some kind of 'running towards.'

Mild intoxication dwindled as the evening came on, and a cold wind seeped in off the sea. Far off behind the distant mountains a white glow rose: the pregnant D of a waxing moon. It lifted its head out of a mass of clouds that were building up in the east. Perhaps the island was finally going to get the rain it so desperately needed? Sushila hung out the last of the tea-towels that she'd rinsed in her dirty wash water and looked again. The clouds billowed up faster than the moon could rise, and it was already partly swallowed. The last lights of the sun had long since faded behind the hill, and it too was beginning to be obscured by cloud. About time for a break in the weather.

Sushila turned to go in and jumped, her hand going to her mouth. "Oh, you startled me."

Dougie bowed slightly, an oddly old-fashioned gesture, and smiled an apology. "I didn't intend to. I hoped we could share a meal again, if you would like to?"

"My place or yours?"

"It will have to be here, I'm afraid. At the moment I can't take you back to my house."

That was okay. Sushila was just pleased to see him, and led the way into the house. Dougie followed her, and she noticed that Flo wasn't trotting at his heels. She was surprised: the dog formed such a part of her mental image of the man, it seemed strange to see him on his own. He looked tired, too, as she laid the table and heated soup. She wondered what work he was doing that could leave him looking so drained.

While she set out the bowls of soup and a heel of bread, he reached into his pocket and pulled out a muslin-wrapped packet, which turned out to contain a soft, white cheese. It made the perfect accompaniment to thick lentil soup and slightly stale bread.

"Mmm, this is yummy," she said around a mouthful of bread and cheese. "Is it locally made? I've never tasted anything quite like it."

"I make it myself," he said, "from sheep's milk."

"You're a man of many talents." He smiled modestly and shrugged the compliment away, but she pressed him. "I mean it. You seem very self-sufficient. Is that a lifestyle choice? Have you tucked yourself away here to escape from the bad old consumer world? Although… you did tell me you grew up here with your grandmother. So did you learn your skills from her?"

He listened patiently to the headlong rush of questions.

"I don't really think about it," he said. "I just get on with things. I did grow up here, but I've never been away, so I don't know what the rest of the world is like."

"You're joking. Dougie, you don't know what you're missing. Do you really mean you've never left this island in your life?"

"I've never left this hill," he said, turning his head to watch the moon flickering between rags of cloud.

Sushila laughed. "Come on, you must have gone to the shops at some point. The bank? School?" She was treating his comments with humour, but he seemed to be completely serious. It didn't make sense.

"School was round on the other side. It was only a roll down the hill from home. There's a village shop there, too. I went to the town, long ago, but I don't need to anymore."

Sushila stared at him, trying to understand. "Dougie, sometimes you sound as if you come from another century. Not even the last one, either. And another thing: I went all over the hill yesterday. I couldn't find any trace of you or your house. Are you on the next hill over? Or did I get myself confused again?"

Dougie nodded, wearily. "You won't find my house at the moment. I told you, I couldn't take you there right now."

Well, that was cryptic. He rose slowly and began to clear the dirty dishes. He leaned on the table for a moment, then levered himself upright with a visible effort. Sushila's curiosity subsided in a wave of compassion. "Sit down," she said. "You look terrible."

"I don't feel great." He sat down at the table and put his head down on his arms.

She finished clearing and walked around behind him, to begin kneading his shoulders. They were hard with tension, but as she massaged they relaxed a little and he sighed. His muffled voice emerged from his folded arms, "Did you make the soup with the spring water?"

"No, the tap's running almost completely dry now. I brought in a supply of bottled water from the shop."

"That's a relief. I thought something had gone badly wrong. Even more wrong than it's going anyway."

Sushila sat down next to him and rested her hand on the back of his neck. "What is going wrong? Can I help?"

Dougie raised his head and looked at her. The moon shining behind him made a silver halo of his rough, unkempt hair. In its ethereal glow his skin looked almost translucent, and for a moment she was reminded of her father fading quietly in his hospital bed, the life perceptibly ebbing from his face. She gasped and put her hand to her mouth. This was an immense contrast to the strong, healthy man who'd whisked her across the stream and into his home. She got up to turn on the light, but a gesture from him stopped her. "Please leave the light off," he said. "It hurts my head. May I have a drink of water?"

She reached for the plastic bottle next to the sink, but again he stopped her. "I need water from the spring," he said.

"I told you, it's not running."

He stood up slowly, the effort clearly costing him, and walked to the tap. When he turned it on there was no response. He held out a hand to her. "Please help me."

Sushila stood and went to him. She put her arms around his waist and rested her head on his chest. "What do you need?" she asked him.

He didn't speak, but laid one hand on her head and with the other turned the tap again. There was a faint, whistling breath. (*From the pipes? Or was it from him?*) The tap emitted a choking noise, and a thin trickle of dark water. It ran just long enough to half fill a glass, then stopped with a wheeze. Sushila's legs buckled and she felt suddenly faint. Her sight darkened, and she felt him take her weight.

When her vision cleared she found herself sitting on a kitchen chair, bent forward with her head between her legs. Dougie was crouched in front of her, with one hand on her wrist and the other holding the glass of dirty water, which he was sipping as though it was the best single-malt whisky. He stroked her cheek and smiled.

"Welcome back."

"What happened? I feel as though I almost fainted."

"Yes, that's what it looked like."

She still felt very strange, but he'd definitely cheered up. He filled the kettle from the plastic bottle and began to make tea. The moon slipped behind a cloud and she noticed that he was looking much more solid. What she thought she'd seen before—that must have been an odd effect of the moonlight. She got up and turned on the kitchen light, banishing the outside world to the blank panel of the window.

Dougie handed her a mug of tea and she cradled it in both hands, which were still white and cold. The colour was back in his face, and she was halfway to convincing herself it had all been in her imagination when he spoke again. "You were right, by the way. As good as the best single malt. In fact, if I'd remembered my hip flask I wouldn't have got into that trouble."

Her mouth fell open. *I didn't say that out loud.* "Dougie MacLean, you read my mind."

"Yes. Or anyway, at a moment like that I can feel the thoughts that are on the surface of your mind. Which comes to the same thing, I suppose."

"A moment like what?" Sushila couldn't decide whether to be scared or intrigued. Things were becoming even more surreal. Dougie took her by the elbow and steered her into the living room. He sat her down on the sofa and perched himself next to her, staring earnestly into her confused eyes.

"I'm going to tell you something, after which you may want me to leave. But I don't want to hide it any longer."

"Look, if you're an axe murderer I'd rather you just left and didn't tell me." Sushila's attempt at a joke fell flat, but she reached forward and gripped his arm. "Spit it out, my lad. I'd rather have bad news than stay confused, and right at the moment you could tell me you were a vampire and it wouldn't surprise me."

He looked bemused and she felt anger well up in her.

"What, never heard of vampires?" He shook his head. "I suppose Bram Stoker never made it to your hill?"

"I'm sorry, Sushila. I really don't know what you're talking about."

She looked at his miserable face and relented. "A vampire is an undead being that gets its life by biting living people and sucking their blood. It's a purely fictional construct, although there are vampire bats in Central and South America that do suck blood. I'm sorry, I didn't mean to imply that you were some kind of supernatural being that cheats death by sucking the life out of people. Obviously, that isn't possible. Also, it was rude. Forgive me?"

"Wait until I've finished telling you. Then it'll be up to you to decide whether forgiveness is appropriate. I haven't been clear with you, and I want that to stop."

"Okay, Mr Mysterious, tell me everything. I promise I'll listen. You've been a good friend so far, and I don't make snap judgments."

He nodded and began to speak. "I am Dougie MacLean. I did grow up with my grandmother, in a house on this hill. I died in 1953."

He paused, and she stared at him open-mouthed. He flinched at the look on her face, and his body stilled as if preparing itself for flight, but he kept speaking.

"I remember my boyhood, running wild on the hill. All the things I told you about: lambs, deer, school, my grandmother. When I grew up I started caring for the sheep, and Gran who was pretty old by then. My brother was normal enough. He went away, first on the local ferry, then into the merchant navy. He always did want to get away. I knew your great-grandmother when she was at school. Her best friend was the girl who would become my wife, Maire."

He paused and hung his head, waiting for rejection, but Sushila was far too curious to let him stop.

"You're telling me you're a ghost."

"Not exactly. It's more complicated than that."

"I'll say it's more complicated. For a start I can see you. And touch you. And I'm quite sure that was real food you fed me in your house, and brought here today." She looked into his worried face and waited until he met her eye, then leaned forward impulsively and kissed his cheek. "You feel real enough to me, Dougie MacLean. But let's say that I trust you. Tell me more about your life. Make me believe it."

She wriggled round and leaned back against him, putting her feet up again on the table, and pulled his arms around her. "I suppose I ought to be afraid, but you've been nothing but kind to me so far. I don't believe you want to harm me. I'll listen to whatever you want to tell me. Just make it good."

He sighed and leaned back into the sofa cushions, his arms tightening on hers. She patted his thigh and closed her eyes, letting the sound of his voice wash over her.

1897

The boy lay on his stomach on a large, flat rock that was almost completely buried in the dusty earth. His bare feet, waving gently in the air behind him, were black with grime, and his soles wore a horny coating of toughened skin. He wore short trousers and a woollen jersey at least two sizes too big for him, with the sleeves rolled up above the elbow. The jersey was knitted mostly in the black wool of the ubiquitous Hebridean sheep, but there were random blotches of grey or white wool mixed in with the black. The ribbed hem at the back was frayed, and a long thread hung down between his legs and brushed the rock. He was no older than two or three.

All his attention was directed at the ground in front of his nose. Ants had established a colony under the flat rock, and the ground was covered with small, black bodies. He held a stem of grass in one hand, and was using it to probe under the edge of the rock, pulling it out to reveal larger ants clinging to its end. Every now and then, one of the soldier ants would run up onto the boy's arm and attach its mandibles to his flesh. Each time, he broke off his probing to brush away the attacker, while keeping his gaze firmly fixed on the drama unfolding below him.

An interrogative sound came from behind him, and the boy answered it, absently. "I found ants, Mam." He spent another minute probing. "They is bitey ones."

"*Trobhad an seo, a bhalaich*," came the voice. And again, after a few minutes, "Come here, boy."

He stood up, brushing ants from his legs and arms, and turned to look at the woman. His eyes shone, vivid and bright, out of a face as dirty as his feet and clothing, and he scratched an insect bite on his leg as he regarded her. Seated in the lee of the blackhouse, out of the hot summer wind that gusted round the corner of the hillside, she paused in her work to gaze down at her son. The boy resembled her, in the curve of his jaw and the slant of his cheekbones. Her face was lined and weathered, but her eyes were clear, and when she smiled she suddenly looked very young.

Her faded woollen dress had once mirrored the dark shades of the boy's jersey, but the fabric was thin and grey from long use and she seemed almost to fade into the stone fabric of the house wall behind her. In one hand she held a spindle, which she dropped and caught repeatedly. The other dipped into one of the large pockets of her apron, drawing out scraps of sheep's wool and feeding them into the spindle thread as it spun.

The boy came to her side and leaned against her, resting his head on her lap. He rubbed his nose on her apron, leaving a trail of snot behind, and mumbled into her thigh. The woman ignored him as she pulled the last wisps of wool from her pocket and wound it onto the spindle. She tucked the spindle into the pocket and bent to drop a kiss on the boy's head. He looked up at her again, trustingly, and she ran one hand through his hair, tenderly stroking the curls that framed his face.

"Fetch your old Mam a cup of water, will you?" she said.

The boy looked up at her, thumb in his mouth, and rubbed an eye with his fist. She regarded him sternly and after a moment he complied. His bare feet made nothing of the stony path—he was obviously accustomed to not wearing shoes—and he trotted away down the hill.

The woman bent forward a little and coughed. The cough was juicy, and clearly painful. She turned to one side and hawked a gobbet of spit onto the stone slab. It glistened scarlet in the summer sunlight. A scrawny dog crept round the side of the house and ate the blood-soaked morsel, then turned away at a whistle from further down the valley. The woman folded her hands in her lap and waited, eyes closed and face turned up to the sun.

8
☽ MAIRE FANNON ☾

"Maire was the prettiest girl in school. Smart, too—even an ignorant school-hater like me could see she was clever—but at the start of the twentieth century there wasn't much point in cleverness for girls. They were only going to grow up, get married and have babies. And in the meantime, there was her dad to take care of, and the little brothers. Her mum had died giving birth to the youngest, so Maire took over the household. It was what you did.

"They lived away, on the edge of the town, though the town was much smaller in those days and their croft was still quite isolated. I used to go over there and help out with the chores. Even when I was quite small I adored her. I always knew I was going to marry her. She used to laugh and hit me over the head. 'Dougal MacLean, you are the end. Fetch me a bucket of water and get on back to your gran before I tell her what nonsense you talk.'

"I left school the first chance I got, but she kept going, started to teach the wee ones, while the school master tutored a couple of older boys for scholarships. I'd be away on the hill all day, drystone walling while I watched the sheep, or learning from Gran. She taught me how to make the sheep's milk cheese, how to bake bread. Almost all the skills that I use to get by, I learned from her, and on Sundays after church I would walk out with Maire Fannon.

"Her father didn't like it. He wanted better for her than a shepherd boy with no parents and no prospects. He wasn't happy that Gran was a wise woman, either, but we went to church like everyone else, there was nothing he could say about that.

"But what better could there be for Maire? She would marry a crofter or a shepherd. There wasn't anything else, unless she wanted to run away to the town and be picked up by a fisherman, or worse. Her father couldn't leave the croft to her, it was meant for her brothers. So whoever she married was going to take her away, to a life neither better nor worse than the one she was living at home."

Dougie stared blankly over the top of Sushila's head. He absently stroked her arms with his long fingers as she rested against him. She let her cheek rest against his upper arm, offering him the comfort of her presence.

"In the end, she came to me. One day Gran lay down beside the stream and died, as quietly as she'd lived, and the whole community came together to mourn her and lay her to rest. She'd helped a lot of families over the years, and her knowledge was valued, even though there was the odd mutter of 'witch' when one man or another was in his cups, Maire's dad included.

"I came home from the hill the next evening and Maire was there, making up a batch of bread in the embers. She told me her dad had taken another wife. 'One woman in a house is enough,' she said; which for someone as strong minded as Maire was probably true. I told her she was lucky she didn't have any sisters, if she felt that way, but she rapped me on the knuckles with the ladle and told me to wash my hands if I expected to get anything to eat. The next Sunday they read the banns at church, and a few weeks later we were married. Her father didn't make any trouble. I expect he was pleased to be rid of her, the new wife in a new bonnet looking very happy beside him.

"I'd never been so happy. Every morning I would wake to her warm body beside me, and climb out into the cold with my piece tucked into my jerkin. At midday I'd take it out and eat it, thinking I could smell her scent on the muslin cloth she'd wrapped it in. At nightfall I'd go home to a hot meal, a warm house: her hand in everything, making it good for me. My young wife, tumbled on the hearth stones in her dusty gown, telling me to stop, was this how respectable folk behaved? And then giving in, with little sighs of pleasure, as I touched her and whispered in her ear, 'You're mine to love now. You could have married into respectable folk, but you chose… this.'"

Sushila, leaning back against Dougie's warm body, felt the unmistakable heat of his erection against her back. Her lower body flooded with warmth in response, and she wriggled. Dougie sat up straighter and subsided, and she relaxed against him again, but a kernel of fire persisted, deep inside her abdomen. This certainly didn't feel like a ghost story.

"The baby was due in March. Maire spent the winter spinning and knitting, all the colours of fleece that I gathered off bushes and thorns each day. She was knitting for me. I told her she should be thinking of the baby, but she said that the new wife had thrown out all the little things carefully kept after her brothers had grown up. She'd been down there and taken the lot, so the baby was taken care of. It was her man who needed warm things. I'd never been so warm before that winter.

"She had a knack of weaving all the shades together as she made her patterns, and each jersey was as warm as three. I kept the shorn fleece from one lamb, even though I needed all the money I could save in case we had to call for the doctor. It was so fine, she couldn't resist it. She made the baby's first gown out of it, and a shawl for herself that would do for a swaddling cloth when the time came, but everything else that came from her hands was for me.

"I was out on the hill when it started. I don't know how long she'd laboured on her own when I reached home. Perhaps the whole day. She was lying on the hearthstones in a pool of her own blood. The bairn lay beside her, already cold. I wrapped her up in all the warm things I could find, and staggered down the hill with her in my arms. The doctor was home, and he took her in and laid her out in the back parlour, on a table. She was still breathing, very shallowly, but he said there was nothing he could do.

"I sat there in that cold, dark room listening to her breathing grow fainter, trying not to make a sound, fearing that each breath was her last. She held on until first light, but as I saw the grey fingers of morning touch her face I realised she was dead.

"The village women had already been up to the house and taken the bairn, and scrubbed the hearth stones clean. My woman and my wee son were buried in the churchyard, and they buried my soul with them. I went back to my hill, but the heart was gone out of me. I got on with the business of living—it's what you have to do—but there was no joy in it for me anymore."

Sushila's fingers tightened on the arm that held her, and she pressed a voiceless message of support into his skin. His muscles were rigid under her hands, as Dougie spoke on in heartbreakingly matter-of-fact tones.

"Another thirty seven years I lived in that house, tending the sheep and making do for myself. I kept the last of her knitting safe in the hope chest, along with the tiny things she'd made for the baby. In the end, I grew so weary of life that all I wanted was to join her again.

"I knew I was ill. My hands and feet were blue all the time and the purpleness had started to spread up my legs. It became a struggle to get myself back up the hill from town, so I stopped going down for supplies. I didn't need much, anyway."

He sighed. "It's a sin to kill yourself, but there's no sin in stopping the work of trying to live. So I opened my house to the elements and took myself up the hill to watch the sun set. I lay down by the head of the spring that fed my valley, and fell asleep in the cold.

"I don't know how much time passed, but when I woke I was as you see me now. Young. Whole. I walked back down the streamside until I came to the house. The roof was gone, and its contents scattered to the wind. It was as if I'd slept for years. Maire was still in my memory, but distant, like a dream from long ago.

"I found I didn't need to eat—just drinking from the spring was enough—and I could sleep out in the frost and take no harm. I rebuilt the house and took up the ordinary tasks of life again, because it felt like the right thing to do. I didn't say the word 'ghost' to myself. I felt alive, no different to my thirties and forties, as if I'd been made young again. I found myself dreaming other lives, too, each as real as my own, the lives of folk whose stories began and ended here on the hill. It was confusing. I felt I'd gone mad, to have changed so utterly in the work of a moment. I didn't understand it.

"I went down towards the town, but I couldn't reach it. Whenever I tried to leave my hill I felt weak and sick, and had to go back. Gradually I've learned my limits, and I've realised I can travel a short distance from the hill so long as I carry some spring water with me. I borrowed the skills I'd watched my brother display, and learned to make my own whisky with water from the spring. But it was my grandmother who told me what I'd become.

"She too was in my mind, because she'd died there on the hill, and more than that. It was to do with her being a wise woman. She tried to teach me when I was alive, but I didn't want to listen. She came to me and told me: I am not just Dougie MacLean. I am all the folk who have died on the hill. My life is tied to the spring; it's the wellspring of my existence. So long as I'm in contact with its water I will live, but I can never go away."

Sushila stirred, and turned round to look at him. Somewhere during the recital of his life she'd stopped disbelieving. Something about his story, the sincerity of his love for his young wife, the details he'd been telling her. Bizarrely, she found it acceptable to believe that he had lived and died generations before she was born. Even so, the living man sat in front of her, visibly willing her to believe in him.

"But your spring is up on the hill. Why did you need my water?"

"A few years after I came back to life, there was a terrible drought. The spring dried up completely. I don't know exactly what happened, in the heart of the mountain, because I died again with it. It wasn't a terrible death. I felt myself fading away, getting thinner and thinner until there wasn't enough left to hold onto. When I woke the spring was running again, but it had changed its course. Now it emerges from the other side of the hilltop and runs down beside your house. So your spring *is* my spring."

"But I've been to your house. I saw the stream up there, and the spring that feeds it."

"You came to the hill in the mist, on a day when I was feeling strong. You saw my house as I see it. I still live in a time when the spring fed the stream in my valley, and everything was green. It's not like that now."

"So was it coincidence that I came across the hill in the mist that day, when something hidden was able to be seen?"

"There must be something special about you, Sushila. I've seen living folk pass across my hill, many times. They are like wraiths in the mist, not solid at all, but you were as warm and living as my own woman. More than that, you've brought me into your world, and it feels as real to me as it does to you. It's more than just the fact that you live in this house. I could see your father, too, when he lived here, but I would not have been able to talk to him. And your mother was a pale shadow; we didn't inhabit the same world."

"I was conceived here," Sushila said. "Mum told me once. Her Scottish author-hero brought her here, to his fairy tale place, took her up the hill and bathed her in water from the spring. He told her she was a fairy wife and he wanted to claim her and keep her with him. It's the myth from one of his novels: they were playacting the parts he'd written. She always told me my life began that night."

Dougie nodded, looking happier. "That makes a kind of

sense, I suppose. It's true you're the first living person I've been able to speak to, and touch. After the first few weeks of my second life, I didn't try. I was content in my solitude. If it didn't get any less lonely, after a while it just became what it was. Life, on some level. Since meeting you, though, I've felt different, as if all this living ought to be for a purpose.

"I feel as though I was given another life for a reason. Maybe it was only that the spring needed to personify itself, like some old legend, but in that case, why Dougal MacLean? It could have been anyone in all the thousands of years the spring has been here. What was the difference that only I could make? Because in all my years of awareness, I've never been able to figure that one out."

He paused, and bent his head to kiss the top of hers. This time the brush of his mouth on her hair was palpable. The grip of his hands on her wrists was warm and strong. It was almost impossible to believe that the man before her was not a living, breathing being. Sushila stood up and pulled him to his feet, planting her feet a shoulder width apart and pointing a finger at his breast bone.

"So you're more than a ghost. More than a man? Yes," she answered her own question. "A man who has lived before, and finds himself living again. A living personification of the spring. Someone who lives through the memories of all those who have died here on the hill. Definitely supernatural." She cocked her head and remarked. "A god?"

"No, not at all. No. Nothing like that."

"No supernatural powers, then?"

He looked uncomfortable, and his gaze dropped before her clear-eyed stare.

"What powers?"

He didn't answer.

"Dougie MacLean, you are a vampire."

"No, I swear."

"A water vampire. You needed to touch me before you

could make the tap run, and you needed the spring water from the tap to keep yourself corporeal. You were fading away in the dry evening air. I saw the moonlight through your skin. Tell me I'm not right."

He nodded reluctantly. "As soon as you told me what a vampire was I recognised the similarity, to my shame. I am not an evil being. I would never take life to feed my own."

"But you could, though, couldn't you? Could you take all my life from me, to pump up your own?"

He was still avoiding her eyes. Her voice cracked like a whiplash in the air between them. "Answer me!"

"Yes." His voice was only a whisper, but he pulled himself up and looked her straight in the eye. "Yes. But I swear on my honour that I would never do it."

Sushila was excited. "Wow. This is amazing. Do it again."

He looked stunned. "What?"

"Take energy from me. I want to see how it works."

"No. Don't you remember how it felt? You almost fainted."

"But I'm ready this time. And anyway, I feel as if I have enough energy for ten people."

He looked thoughtful. "I think that's a side effect of what I do. You have an intimate association with the spring. It must be what allowed me to make contact with you in the first place, and even though it's low at the moment, you have still been drinking from it, and visiting the source. Some of me is running in your veins, so that although I took energy from you to stabilise myself, you benefit as I do from my growing strength. Most likely you'd feel a brief loss of strength, followed by a massive surge of energy."

He paused, thinking. "I took from you that day on the hill, to make it all substantial enough to hold you. Did you feel that?"

"I was so tired and sore when I met you, I didn't expect to feel better any time soon. It wouldn't have surprised me that I carried on feeling that way, but the next morning my leg was amazingly improved. I've never recovered so quickly from a spell of pain. Dougie, I've got enough energy to fuel a cascade, and you look deathly. Come here."

She stepped forward and wrapped her arms around his waist, then reached up towards him. Dougie turned his head away, but she took his face in her hands and turned him back to face her. On tiptoes she pressed her lips gently against his.

For a second or two he resisted, then crushed her against him and kissed her hard. As he pulled back she put out her tongue and touched his top lip with its moisture. He groaned, and she felt the room spin. A grey mist briefly blurred the edges of her vision, and her knees gave way, but he held her and soon enough the dizzy feeling cleared away. Dougie picked her up and kissed her soundly again. His eyes were bright and shining, and he laughed for sheer joy.

"How do you feel?" he asked her.

"I feel fantastic."

1901

Across the uplands the wind screamed, its full force buffeting the two figures that made their way across the landscape, dwarfed by the power of nature unleashed. Storms in springtime are a different beast to the grim, fell tempests of winter. The mixing of winds in the upper atmosphere that coincides with the equinox can bring a weather event whose ferocity is all the more surprising for coming so swiftly on the heels of daffodils, spring grass, apple blossom—and new-born lambs.

The boy crouched lower to the ground, cringing into the poor shelter of the man's stooped body. Gusts snaking across the cotton-grass threatened to lift him off his feet, and he clung to his father. The man, in turn, bent almost double by the wind, appreciated the small but determined lump of ballast attached to his coat-tail.

Over the brow of the hill, they turned a corner and the worst of the wind fell away. The man still did not stand fully upright; the zone of shelter was no higher than a few feet above the ground, and above it ice-pellets and stinging gobbets of sleet shot past horizontally. On the floor of the hollow, looking to be no more than a tumbled grey-and-white mass, lay a sheep.

The man crouched, dragging the boy with him, one hand still wrapped in the corner of his father's coat, the other coming up now to insert its thumb into his mouth. He stood watching, aware of nothing more than a sense of respite from the wind and the comfort of his father's presence. He wondered if the ewe was dead.

As his father hauled the sheep over it stirred, briefly kicking one leg. It let out a breath, but did not bleat. The man examined it, opening its eyes and mouth, and then groping into the mass of the wool to find its nether regions.

"This one's sinking fast," he said. The boy stood numbly, not responding. This wasn't the first moribund animal they had found tonight. The sudden storm had caught many of the ewes unawares. Some had aborted spontaneously, and left their not-quite-ready offspring behind them to be cleaned up by eagles and ravens. Others went into labour, and failed in the process. For ewe and shepherd alike, surviving the birthing process was the important part. They could always be bred again next year. The truly devastating losses for the shepherd were the ewes that died giving birth. Everything was lost then.

The man shook the sheep, and tried to haul it to its feet. Far from objecting, the animal made no response at all. The only sign it was still alive was the occasional sigh that emerged from its mouth. The boys looked on with interest: something had emerged from the rear end of the animal. He tugged at his father's coat. The man looked and let out a guttural phrase of Gaelic. The boy stored this away in his memory for future reference.

"The lamb's breach, and she's doing naught to help it. It's up to us, boy."

He crouched behind the ewe and delved into her fleece. "Come, boy, feel here."

The boy squatted beside his father and curiously touched the foot that protruded from the ewe's fundament.

"We need to get the other foot out. I can't get my hand in there. It's too big. You're going to have to do it."

The boy withdrew the thumb from his mouth and shook his head. The man saw nothing of this gesture in the half-dark of the storm, but he recognised the body language. Swiftly he grabbed the child's hand and forced up into the space between the protruding hoof and the ewe's vaginal wall. The boy grunted in surprise; it was warm in there.

"Now, reach for the other foot." The man's voice was harsh, but encouraging. "Tell me what you feel."

The boy did not reply. With his free hand he braced against the woolly flank. The ewe stirred as a mild contraction rippled through her uterus. The boy winced but did not withdraw his hand. At the full reach of his fingers he could just touch a hard object. Probably that was the foot his father was talking about. He edged himself closer, his whole arm disappearing inside the ewe.

The man spoke soothingly in a low voice to the animal and to the boy. His voice rolled around the hollow, muffled by the shriek of the storm, but the boy had gone beyond its reach. Deep in the warm, red place in which he found himself he grasped the lamb's foot and tried to draw it out.

The ewe grunted and her uterus contracted again, crushing the boy's arm inside the muscular tube. He screamed, but did not let go.

The boy rested his head on the ewe's flank. He could feel the life ebbing in her, drawing a little further away with each breath. Without thought, he began to sing a little, wordless lament under his breath. For a moment, the howl of the wind ceased. The snow stopped swirling past, and fell straight down in heavy clumps. A fog of ice-droplets blew into the hollow and covered them, and in that moment the boy's arm slipped free, along with the second foot, and the ewe's last breath,

With a grunt of satisfaction, the man reached down and grasped the hind legs of the lamb. Boot braced against the sheep, he pulled it free with one sharp action. The lamb hung from his hand, swaying a little in the rising wind.

The man pummelled it, and put his hand into its mouth to draw out a mass of mucus. Weakly, the lamb struggled in his grasp. With his free hand he hauled the boy to his feet.

"No time to rest, boy," he said. "You've a job to do." Pulling up the thick, woollen jersey, he inserted the lamb between the boy's shirt and his skin. "Hold that in there now," he instructed. "If we can keep it going till we get back, it may live."

With one swift movement he hauled the carcass of the

ewe onto his shoulders and turned back to the exposed hillside. One hand again clinging again to the coat, and the other pressing the body of the lamb against his stomach, the boy stumbled behind his father, blinded by rain and darkness. The ewe's body bumped against his father's back with every step, dripping blood and fluids onto the boy's head.

The lamb moved weakly and the boy clung to it tightly, no longer aware of anything outside the circle of his father's steps, the coat he clutched and the living warmth of the thing that lay next to his heart. Behind him the wind roared its anger, buffeting the pair of them from side to side, before as suddenly shifting direction and gusting from a different quarter. The man shouted, and his words were torn away into the night. The boy heard them, though.

"This will blow itself out by morning. And tomorrow? Tomorrow we'll feast, my boy."

9
☽ THE SEA TAKES ☾

Lifting her easily, Dougie swung her round in a circle, and set her back on her feet. "Make tea, woman," he demanded. "It's your turn to put out."

"I beg your pardon?" Sushila stood with her hands on her hips. "What makes you think I'll put out for you? You might think you're special, and come to think of it you are, but—"

"No, I didn't mean that. It's your turn to tell me a story, and I know which one I want."

She rested one hand on the kitchen bench and leaned against it, before turning her back on him and busying herself making tea. For all that she'd made a joke of it, she was sick with desire for him. She couldn't decide how much it was natural attraction, how much her own years of celibate loneliness, and how much the dizzying effect of energy rushing through her body. She felt herself shaking, like a pipe battered from within by the flood water rushing through it. She wanted nothing more than to pull this man down on the cold tiles of the kitchen floor and find out what he was made of.

"Made of water," she muttered to herself, and giggled.

"Pardon?"

"Nothing. Here's your tea. Nothing special about its water, I'm afraid. Feel free to touch me up if you feel the need."

He laughed. "You are full of yourself, all of a sudden."

She stood back and looked him up and down, taking in the whole, desirable length of him from shaggy head and dark eyes to long, slender fingers and down to his feet. "Full of you, more likely, if I understand it."

He sobered, then took her hand and led the way silently back to the living room. He sat on the sofa and she curled up beside him, facing him. He put down his mug and gathered her feet onto his lap, gently massaging her toes. It was an exquisite feeling. Sushila sat sipping her tea and gazed at him.

"Now, *mo nighean*, I need to hear how you came by that leg."

She jerked compulsively, pulling her feet back into her body, but he stroked them gently and persuaded her reluctant muscles to relax. "I know you don't want to tell me. There's enough of me in you to make me certain that the end of the story of your happiest day is an equal and opposite weight of sadness. It's time for you to tell it."

She put down her cup and covered her face with her hands. For a moment she rocked back and forth, speechless, but the gentle warmth of his hands on her legs released her.

"I had such a short time with Alan." Her voice was only a breath, almost inaudible, but he nodded as if he heard every word clearly. He held out his arms to her and she crawled into them. She spoke the rest of the story into the dark space between his arms and the rough wool of his jersey, and if at times her voice trailed into silence, broken with sobs, the story kept on telling itself, wordlessly, until he'd heard it all.

"It was wonderful. We started advertising our surfing lessons straight away. Alan prepared a comprehensive business plan: even Priya was impressed. We wrote together to Mum and Dad, and to his parents, and told them what we were doing. My family put up a surety and the bank agreed to make us a loan to build a small hut on the water's edge. All of a sudden we were running a proper company, with accounts and debts and clients.

"It was a baptism of fire for me, made me realise how bloody lazy I'd been. Over the last weeks of the monsoon he made me study for my exams. He said he didn't want a wife who'd been given opportunities but squandered them. Within a week of the end of the monsoon we'd made enough money to invest in some more gear, and we could begin to teach those who came on holiday with no surf gear at all.

"For a man who'd spent his adolescence cruising the world from one surf beach to another, Alan had an amazing head for business. He knew exactly what he wanted to achieve. By the end of the year he'd already expanded the school into a residential facility. Priya took on some more help, and fed the visitors up in the house, and every morning at dawn we'd have a small army of surfing addicts waxing their boards and looking forward to another day at Alan's mercy. Not one person passed through his hands without radically improving their skills.

"He was as hard on the guests as he was on himself, and me. I found it difficult. There wasn't much time left for romance. But he found his moments: a brush of lips over breakfast, a bump of hips in the surf. Dancing in the dark down on the sand. When at last he made love to me, I thought my heart would break with the wonder of it.

"We set a date for the wedding. It would be the following May, during the monsoon, a sensible business decision, as the school would have to close down anyway for those weeks when the sea was unsuited to surfing. His mum and dad were planning to come over from Australia. My dad sent flowers, and told me he would be proud to give me away. Aby was taking a break from filming and came home for Christmas. And I was pregnant. Too early to show even a bump, but I was being sick every day, all day, and I'd missed two periods. There wasn't any doubt about it. Alan was as proud as a cockerel, couldn't keep his hands off my non-existent bump, made me promise to tell him the moment I felt any movement; he wanted to feel his son for himself.

"I couldn't get excited over it all. I just felt too ill. On

Boxing Day morning I got up early and set off with Priya. She wanted to take me to a little shrine in the hills which she believed held healing powers that would help me. I didn't believe a word of it, but it made Priya happy and I wasn't sleeping anyway, so I might as well follow her guidance. Couldn't make things any worse."

The words dried up in her throat. She lifted her head and looked at the man who held her calmly and quietly. His eyes communicated support as he bent forward to set a gentle kiss on her forehead. Tears streamed down her face but she gathered herself together and crawled back into his embrace.

"We made an offering at the shrine, and drank some water blessed by a local saint. Then we started to make our way back. I've gone over the next moments over and over again in my mind. Aby would have been sitting out in the sun, taking in some early rays after breakfast. Alan would have been going over the books; we were due to make a payment on the bank loan, and I know that he was obsessed with getting every detail right.

"The first wave probably reached all the way up to the top of the foredunes, but because there was a small rise of land concealing their view of the sea, they would have had no idea of what was on the way until the second wave struck. Priya and I were higher up the road, and we saw it coming. We turned to run but it was moving incredibly fast. We were swept apart from each other, and I saw her body sucked under a lorry that was floating past. I tried to grab onto things, but it was like being in a washing machine full of debris that battered me and forced me under. Eventually, it spat me out with my left leg broken in three places, half-conscious and vomiting sea water. Someone must have taken me to a hospital. I woke up with my leg in plaster and the last cramps of miscarriage thrusting through my body.

"I was one of the lucky ones. I was surrounded by people groaning in misery, many with injuries much worse than mine. The worst thing was the children. The school in our little town was safely up on the hill, and many of the kids were on their way to school when the wave struck. So there were suddenly hundreds of frightened, injured children crying their hearts out, and no-one to take care of them because their parents were all dead.

"The hospital staff did their best. The building wasn't damaged, as it stood on a ridge of high ground, but it was overrun by waves of injured and dying people. Something went wrong when they set my leg, and it became infected. In the end, I had to endure a series of operations to clean out the wounds and reset the bones.

"Eventually, aid began to trickle in. I was fed a huge dose of antibiotics, and the wounds began finally to heal. As I say, I was one of the lucky ones. Dad came and found me and took me back to England, where I received the all clear, in terms of my physical health, and endured a whole lot of physiotherapy. The results of that you can see: with some restriction I can walk again. And this is what I was left with."

She pulled up her trouser leg to show him the long, puckered scars, the misshapen calf with half its muscle missing. He made no comment, and she let the fabric slide down again.

"When I finally pulled myself together I asked Dad to tell me the truth about the others. He showed me photos of the house and surf school. He'd been down there while I was still lying in hospital, too ill to be moved. There was nothing left. Nothing. The little peninsula where Priya had lived, where Aby had been born, where we'd begun to build our lives: it was all swept clean. Alan and my mother were never found. Priya was identified. She still had her shoulder purse around her neck, even though her clothes were stripped away by the wave. Dad paid for her cremation and burial while I was still in the hospital. But Alan and Aby were just gone."

Sushila sat up and scrubbed her eyes with her hands. Her face was lined with remembered pain, all the light gone out of it, the double line between her brows strong and clear.

"Financially, I was fine. We had good international business insurance, Alan had planned for every kind of disaster, so that paid off the bank loan, and we let the land go. What was the point of keeping it? People who lived there needed it. I'd got away. I was okay."

"What about the surf school?" Dougie's voice was low and sympathetic.

"What surf school? That was Alan: always Alan. And I'll never surf again," she said, gesturing again at the leg. "I went back anyway. Worked as a volunteer in one of the orphanages that were suddenly full. All these years and things have still not got back to normal. Parts of the country got better international help than others, and some of what was done was no use to people on the ground.

"Somebody put up a fund to build homes for fishermen who'd lost everything. They were rehoused miles away from the sea, in areas thought to be safe from future tsunamis, but what use was that? They only knew fishing, so they found themselves unemployed. The new settlements were no more than shantytowns for benefit claimants who'd once been proud self-employed men."

Sushila shook her head, tears standing at the corners of her eyes again.

"I felt so guilty. I survived. I was actually wealthier than before, because the money was in the bank and I didn't have to worry about paying the bills anymore. It suited me to bury myself in work, and working at the orphanage felt like some kind of partial payback.

"I was still there in 2009, when the Sri Lankan army brought the Tamil Tigers to bay in the north of the country. That was a terrible time. Even down in the south-west we were affected by refugees trying to escape the fighting, and the news was full of the enemy. Priya's people. My people, whether those around me realised it or not.

"Dad was frantic with fear for me, and I agreed to go home for a while, but when it all settled down again, I went back. I didn't know what else to do with myself. I felt I had to atone for surviving. And I didn't leave again until I got the call to say that he'd had the stroke. Then I found myself dealing with guilt all over again. I wasn't there for him when he needed me, and by the time I got back he was beyond words. I have to live with the knowledge that I ran away, and that my cowardice cost me the chance to become close to my father again. Too late. Too bloody late."

Her voice ran down and stopped, like a clockwork toy that had run out of spring. She looked at Dougie out of a blank, white face, and spoke, her voice flat. "So, now you know. Not a pretty story, I'm afraid. And the leg is nothing, nothing at all, compared to the rest of it."

Dougie gathered her back into his arms and held her. He didn't speak, but rocked her gently, humming deep in the base of his throat; a low sound at the edge of hearing like the slow movement of an underground river. Sushila felt herself cradled in an endless sea of compassion, great enough to swallow all her grief in its bottomless depths. She sighed and relaxed, suddenly boneless, and between one breath and the next sleep swept her into its healing embrace.

1904

The walls of the blackhouse were low and squat. Its thatch hung almost to ground level, held in place by a much-mended fishing net, weighted all around the edge by large stones bound with cord. The boy looked up at the roof, trying to guess the source of the leak.

He'd been woken that morning by rain dripping onto his face. Clearly, there was a gap in the thatch, but by the nature of water the hole need not be anywhere near the place where it had emerged to soak his plaid laid out on the floor. The netting sagged, and the cords were becoming thin. The whole thing could do with renewing; at the very least it needed repair.

As he stood, the boy remembered the day the roof had been laid, the old, mouldy thatch drawn aside to dry, ready to be forked into the lazybeds up on the hill. His father had stood there, ensuring the new roof was secure before throwing the net down to the boys who stood by, ready to tie on the stones in their rope hammocks. In his mind, the boy saw his father proud and tall on the rooftop. "Like a cock on a dunghill," said his grandmother's voice in his mind.

That wasn't the last time he'd seen his father, fine and strong, a proud figure among the other men. Two years later, he and his brother had run down the hill to the town road, to watch the Argyll Highlanders march away to a war in a place they could hardly imagine. Their father stood a head taller than the rest; life with Gran had been good to him, and he'd escaped the malnourishment that had blighted the rest of his generation following the clearances.

His father looked smart and cheerful in the MacLean

tartan, happy to be going away. After all, what was there for him here? A dead wife, two puling bairns and the *cailleach*, wrinkled as a prune and ancient as time. She'd refused to come down and see him off: he'd made his farewell to her the day before.

"I could do with that song, old woman," he said to her, a look of mischief in his eyes. "In case some Campbell takes a shot at me in the heat of battle."

She wore a look of patient contempt. "You're leaving me, laddie," she said to him. "You've given me all you have to give. And I have nothing more to give you."

He shrugged and grinned, pulling his pack onto his back and ruffling the hair of the younger boy. "Aye, well, and you're welcome to them," he said.

It took many months before the boy realised that his grandmother had been talking about him, and his brother. They were all his father had to give her. By that time he knew his father wasn't coming back.

"Hold your dreaming, boy," said his grandmother. Her hand caught him a hard blow on the back of the head and he started. The thatch was grubby and unkempt, and it was many years since it had been properly maintained. He looked round at his grandmother and opened his mouth, but she interrupted him.

"No, *a ghràidh*. You're not to do it. Wait till your brother gets home."

He knew perfectly well his brother was no more likely to climb that roof than his grandmother herself, but he held his tongue. Down the slope he could see a figure walking towards them. A young woman, accompanied only by the basket she held over one arm. A pretty woman dressed in the fashion of town.

"Round the back with you now," Gran said. "Get the byre cleared out. Quietly, mind. Keep the ears open and the mouth closed, aye?"

"Aye." He ducked to avoid a second skelping and made

his way quickly round to the back half of the dwelling. Inside, old Bessie stood patiently in the darkness. They'd only today sold her calf to the factor's lad, for fattening on the good land down by the loch. It was one of the few things they could sell for money, but the money itself had to be hoarded against the cost of getting the cow serviced again next year. In the meantime, her milk was a precious commodity. Turned into cheese, it could be traded for many of the things they couldn't make themselves.

He reached into his jerkin and pulled out a pad of warm, wilted grasses. The cow, smelling the fresh fodder, bunted him with her head. He led her to the manger and dropped the grass in. He left her there, comfortably lipping at the treat, as he fetched the broom and began to brush the rank straw and droppings into a pile, ready to put out onto the potato beds. He paused as he heard the sound of voices, low at first and then clear as the two women entered the human side of the house.

He hunkered down on his heels and prepared to listen. His grandmother would quiz him on whatever he heard, be it a tedious request for a love potion, or more interesting problems such as the pox or an unwanted baby. If she was satisfied with his recollection, this time she might agree to teach him the song she'd forbidden his father. *I am not here; there is nothing to see.* The refrain ran through his mind, and he could almost feel the shape of the tune. But it wouldn't work unless she gave it to him whole.

Old Bessie sighed and let go a whoosh of grass-scented wind. Breathing the comfortable stench of the cow's digestion the boy made himself comfortable and set his mind to remember.

10
☽ WHISKY AND WATER ☾

When Sushila woke she was in her own bed, wrapped up in the duvet. She rolled over and put her bare feet out onto the cold boards of the floor. She wandered through the house, but there was no sign of the man. He'd left her a note on the kitchen table, written on the back of her shopping list. The letters were neat, but painstaking. She could read the truth of his discomfort with writing in every careful pen stroke. Only his initial curved exuberantly, like the moon half full.

Come to the spring. I will meet you if I can. D.

She felt clear-headed and light on her feet, as if a great, grey cloud of misery had been washed away with the rising sun. Outside, the yellow disk glared down on a world becoming drier with every moment. The hopeful clouds of the night before had come to nothing. There'd be no rain today.

She made breakfast and ate it slowly, feeling as though the day portended great things and she should approach it with solemnity, but by the time she'd finished eating her natural impetuosity asserted itself. She filled the pack with sandwiches, snacks and drinks and headed out the door, snatching up her walking poles and heading straight for the spring. The dry air rasped at her mouth as she climbed, pushing herself for the sheer pleasure of it, overriding the twinges from her leg until she reached her goal, where she threw herself down next to the springhead and panted, feeling her pulse pounding in her ears. When it finally began to settle she sat up and looked out across the view.

In the hazy, purple distance all the mountains on the mainland bar the tallest had lost any trace of snow. The fields falling away before her were yellowing and sere, and the upturned blue porcelain bowl of the sky was clamped firmly upon the horizon. The wind sweeping up the hill was bitterly cold, and contained no hint of moisture. Sushila looked around, but there was no sign of Dougie. If he was as tied to the spring as he claimed, she couldn't imagine how it would be possible for him to come to her, even here at the source.

She lay down on her stomach and put her head down into the hollow of the spring. Under its mossy lip the space still held a hint of moisture, and there was a gleam of water between the stones. She reached down a hand and touched a fingertip to one of the shining puddles. At her hip, her mobile phone vibrated and rang.

She sat up and answered it. A faint hiss, like the sound of the sea in a coiled shell. Then, as if coming from a great distance, his voice. "Sushila?"

"Dougie? I thought you didn't have a phone."

"I don't.'

'How are you calling me?"

"Manipulation of electromagnetic radiation."

"Ha ha. Very funny. Do you even know what that is?"

"Come to me and we can argue about it." There was a note of impatience in his voice, and a silent pause as if the connection had been lost.

"Hello? Are you there? What should I do?"

"Start walking. I'll tell you when you're close."

Putting aside her indignation at a partner who could call her phone despite not owning one himself, yet apparently couldn't give coherent directions, she pulled herself to her feet and picked up the poles. Striking upward, she turned in the direction she'd taken when looking for the spring with such dismal lack of success the other day.

As she began to walk, the voice whispered in her ear. "Go left a little…walk forward…now go down."

Following intermittent instructions that murmured at the very edge of hearing, she wandered round the edge of the hill. Scrambling down a dry scree slop, she came into a little hollow with the hint of a cave towards its back. As she neared it, she realised that it was partly walled with stones, and behind it was a dark, cool space from which issued a moist scent redolent of peat bogs and rot: pungent and earthy, but not unpleasant. Dougie stood in the opening, waiting for her.

He held out his arms and she walked into them, appreciating his cool touch on her skin. Then she pulled her head back and glared at him. "So, explain to me: why do you not have a phone?"

"I've never needed to call anyone before. Didn't know I could. Anyway, if I had a phone wouldn't the battery run flat? You seem to be forever charging yours."

"Listen, mate, if you can call me on the airwaves without a handset, I'm sure you can work out how to charge a battery in a thunderstorm or something. At least up here you'll always have a signal."

"I suppose you're right. Just because I haven't adopted modern technologies, doesn't mean that I can't use them. Anyway," he continued primly, "it's very nice to see you."

"Yes, it is, isn't it?" And she put up her mouth to be welcomed with a kiss. He tasted of berries, and spring water, and… "Whisky!"

"Welcome to my still," he said, laughing at the expression on her face.

The back of the enclosure was dominated by an enormous still, beside which were piled several dozen wooden casks. On a stone lip jutting from the wall at his shoulder stood a dusty, green bottle. He lifted and wiped it, then handed it to her. She raised the cool glass to her lips and took a mouthful. "Oh my Lord," she wheezed.

"Well, they don't call it the water of life for nothing."

"Damn right." The next mouthful went down as smooth as chocolate, but it left behind a smouldering fire from her throat all the way to her stomach. "That's good stuff."

They spent the rest of the day sitting with their backs against the still, taking turns at the bottle. Along the way they managed to eat all the sandwiches, and work their way through the titbits she'd tucked into her pack. At one point they fought over the last biscuit. Gasping with laughter, covered with crumbs where he'd taken his winnings and crumbled them over her face, she poked him in the chest. "For a guy who doesn't need to eat, you seem to be quite keen on food."

"You've reminded me of the value of appetite."

They looked at each other, then he reached for her and they began to kiss. She wriggled her bottom in the dust, trying to squirm closer to him. In the end he slithered down to the floor and pulled her down on top of him, kissing her in lines of fire from her ear to the point of her shoulder and back again. She pinned his hips between her thighs and ground herself against him, slipping her cold fingers under his jersey and making him hiss as she stroked his ribs. By the time they pulled apart they were both panting, and she felt as though a small volcano had sprung to life in her abdomen.

Sushila was impetuous as always, wanting more, but Dougie was more cautious. He held her off with one strong hand, while the other reached behind him for an earthenware crock tucked away in a corner. He pulled out the cork with his teeth and upended the vessel over her head. A cool drizzle of water flowed over her forehead. Instantly she sobered, while he took a mouthful and careful replaced the stopper. Sushila stood and wiped the moisture from her face, then sucked it from her fingers. It felt slightly fizzy on her tongue, and it held a flavour to which she was beginning to become accustomed. "Spring water," she said.

"All I've got now, until it rains," he said, "but it will be enough."

"How can you be sure? It might stay dry for weeks. The forecasters aren't making any promises."

"I can feel it coming. It's a long way off, to be sure, but it's on its way. The rain will arrive with the full moon, that's what it feels like. Less than a week away, now."

"I hope you're right. The whole countryside is desperate for water. Never mind any supernatural beings that might be lurking in the background."

"I never lurk."

"Says who? I'm sure I spotted you lurking this morning, while I was slogging my way round the hill in the sunlight."

He grinned and pulled her to him; she could smell the warm aroma of sweaty maleness, better by far than any artificial scent. Strangely, there was no smell of whisky. She realised that she was completely sober, as if she'd never been drunk at all. A few drops of the pure spring water had washed away all traces of alcohol from her system. "You could bottle that and sell it as a hangover cure," she said appreciatively. "Make a fortune."

"It wouldn't work on anyone else," he said. "Only us."

Us. She thought about that for a moment.

"Dougie…?"

"Mm…hmm?"

"I am still alive, aren't I? I would know if I'd died in my sleep and come to join you in your second life?"

"You are very much alive," he told her. "The miracle of you is that you have given so much more life to me. With the spring at such a low point, I should be barely conscious. It's thanks to you that I can hold myself together, but you are as alive and whole as the day I met you. Perhaps a little more, I hope."

"What do you mean?"

"It doesn't take a mind reader to see that you've only been half alive since the wave that took your family. It swept away more than your loved ones and your strength; it took your moral courage, but if you're strong enough to give me all that you have done—your strength, your trust, your belief—I think you're capable of healing all the way, and taking back your life."

Sushila was uncomfortable. "I don't want my life back. It's gone. They've all gone. There's nobody left now."

Dougie was brutally straight-forward. "They are dead. You've lost them. But you, my darling, are so alive that you could practically raise the dead. You are capable of astonishing things, if only you believe in yourself."

"Dougie, listen. If I bury Dad's ashes on the hill, will he come back to life in you?"

"Oh, my love." His grasp on her shoulders was suddenly very gentle. "No. He died away from here, and was cremated, so there's nothing of the spring left in him. If you would like to place his ashes here, I would be honoured, but he will not be able to speak to you. He's truly gone."

She was crying again, and he sat on the low wall outside the enclosure and let her lean on him. "Listen, *a nighean*. Of course you may bury him here, if that gives you comfort, but you already know what he wanted."

"He wanted to be with Mum," she blurted. "That's impossible. I can't make miracles happen, no matter what pretty compliments you pay me."

Dougie was calm and practical with her. He gentled her with his hands, and handed out a slightly grubby handkerchief from his jeans pocket. "Where is your mum?"

"Gone… gone, gone, gone! Her body was never found. How many times do I have to tell you?"

"Think again." His voice soothed her. "Where is she now?"

Sushila stopped crying and stared at him. "Somewhere in the Indian Ocean. Off the coast of Sri Lanka." She scrubbed her nose on the sleeve of his jersey and sniffed. "You're right. Dad would have wanted to be with her. That's what I need to do."

"Good girl."

"But I don't want to leave you." Suddenly she sounded like a little girl, lost and frightened. "I don't want to go away."

"Don't panic. Stay with me until the rain comes. I'll be able to give you what strength I possess, and I promise you'll find that you have the will to do what needs to be done."

1906

The school room ought to have been quiet, the only sounds the scratching of the infants' slates as they practised the letter of the day, the quiet murmur of Maire's voice as she worked with the youngest members of the class, and the squeak from the blackboard as the dominie chalked up a series of sums for his older pupils to attempt. It wasn't.

Hugh was coughing again. Dougie could hear it, behind and to his left: the slight intake of breath, the wheezy croak as Hugh tried to hold it in, then the hoarse bark of the cough, and an audible wince of pain from the boy, echoed silently by everyone else in the room.

The dominie paid no heed to the interruption, but he wouldn't long ignore the whisper of voices, faint at first but growing, within which could now be discerned the syllables of one boy's name. Dougie flinched. It was no use. He'd have to say something. He cleared his throat and opened it to speak, but nothing came out.

"Come on, Dougie." Matt's voice crept above the general muttering.

Dougie hunched his shoulders and glanced to his left, where Maire was taking the wee ones through their alphabet. He met her eyes, clear, grey and kind, and his resolve strengthened. His hand shot up. "Please, Sir?"

The dominie ignored him. That wasn't unexpected. He knew better than to call out again, but sat in his seat with his arm pumped straight up above his head. He held it there for a long moment, though not long enough for the fingers to begin to go numb. Hugh, relieved at the sight of his friend and protector's intervention, let go with a sharp barrage of coughs that their teacher could no longer disregard.

The man whirled round, aiming his piece of chalk in the direction of the interruption. At his movement the whole room fell silent, apart from one clear voice reciting "C is for…" before trailing off in embarrassment. The chalk stayed in the man's hand. Hugh was bent double over his desk, red-faced with the effort of controlling the cough. The dominie deigned at last to notice the upstretched hand, now beginning to tremble.

"Boy?" he barked.

"Please, Sir. Hugh is sick again, Sir."

Silence for a moment while the man observed Hugh, as if he'd been completely unaware of the coughing fit. Hugh sat and wheezed quietly.

"I know your intent, boy." He fixed Dougie with an unnerving stare. "You think to escape your sums."

"No, Sir," he dared to answer back. "Perhaps someone could take him home, Sir?"

"Someone, eh?" The terrifying eye moved on and he breathed again. The dominie's glance alighted on Maire, sitting with her hands folded primly in her lap. "You, girl," he said. "Take the boy home. Come straight back. The rest of you: ten minutes recess. Do not leave the schoolyard."

His last instruction was swallowed up in the scraping of chairs and a mass stampede for the door. Hugh smiled gratefully as he stood and Maire offered her arm in support. They shuffled into the playground, and as Dougie exited behind them he could already hear the scratch of the dominie's chalk, adding another sum to the blackboard.

He ran three times round the perimeter of the tiny playground and sank down in the shelter of the stone wall. He could feel a story starting in his head, a new one, and now was his chance to let it rise to the surface; but the infants had other ideas. They gathered round his knees, importuning him with their eyes. "Tell us a story, Dougie. Please." Sighing, he complied.

A few of the bigger boys gathered around, but he wasn't

worried. They wouldn't last long. He chose a story they'd all heard many times before.

"Once upon a time…" The wee ones wriggled in anticipation. "Once upon a time, in the long long ago, there lived a wee man in a ragged coat. His name was Airgiduine, and he lived in the deep dark bottom of the tarn at the top of the Beinn."

"Ooooh." Big Rab pretended to be frightened. "Was it a kelpie? Was it the *Each-Uisge*, that drags travellers into its lake and eats their livers?" He grabbed one of the infants and dug his long fingers into its ribs, displaying a sound knowledge of anatomy, probably gained, like his hard hands, from helping his father with the butchering. The child squealed and giggled: it hurt, but was also very ticklish. Dougie forbore to react.

"It was not."

The older boys, bored, gave up the sport of baby-baiting and ran off to the other side of the schoolyard. As expected. He nodded in satisfaction and continued the story.

"One day, he came down from the mountain, in his ragged trousers and shabby coat, and he found his way to the tailor's house, for more than anything in the world he wanted a new tweed coat, and everyone knew that Tailor MacLeod was the best tailor in the world, and his brother Mack was the best weaver.

"And, as everybody also knows." Dougie paused and eyed his audience. They sat expectantly, eyes fixed on his face. "In the bottom of the deep, dark tarn at the top of the Beinn, Airgiduine had a secret stash of…"

"Silver!" the infants chorused.

In the door of the schoolhouse the dominie stood, the school bell in his hand. Its tuneless clang told out the end of play. The faces of the infants were disappointed as they scrambled to their feet, but no-one complained. Those who hadn't yet felt the sting of the dominie's cane had heard the whistle of it strike another child's hand or leg, and seen the red marks it left behind.

Dougie glanced across the wall: Maire was running, her long plait swinging behind her. He smiled in relief and turned to follow the wee ones inside.

11
☽ EQUINOX ☾

The next few days raced by. Sushila cleared the yard and arranged with Mary to take most of Dad's remaining things to the recycling centre. Another day she trekked into town and lunched once more with her new island friends. She replied to letters from the London agents, and climbed the hill more than once to make phone calls to London. Now, she was making plans for a return visit to Sri Lanka: one last chance to say goodbye, while she scattered Dad's ashes. Then off again, back to Scotland, where she would settle and live this life forever. Happy ever after: who wouldn't want that? And at the end of a long and lovely life, she could lay herself down on the hill and be with Dougie forever.

The first night she spent alone, lying on the sofa with one ear open for the knock at the door. But the wind was drier and colder than ever, and there wasn't even a breath of moisture left at the spring. On the second night, just as she was beginning to accept that she would be alone again, the light touch came at the door and she went to it, to find him standing there in his stockinged feet, boots in one hand and an earthenware flagon in the other. This was a different brew, more like a rich cider than a fully distilled spirit. He claimed it was made with windfall apples and hazelnuts.

"Whatever," she said, half filling a mug and clinking it against his. "*Slàinte mhath*, anyway. And *glé mhath* for good measure."

They sat on the sofa and kissed for a while, until she was drowsy with the slow rise of pleasure, but Dougie wanted to talk. He wanted to hear everything she could tell him about Sri Lanka and slowly, seeing it through his eyes, Sushila began to remember all the things she loved about her home.

"It's very beautiful. People are poor, but there's this wonderful, exquisite beauty to everything you see. So long as there are fish in the sea, and crops to grow, people survive, and they spend their time producing the most beautiful things."

She brought out the batik cloth from the bottom of her father's chest of drawers, and spent an hour telling him the whole process by which it was made. She used it as the basis of her assertion that colours were brighter under the sub-tropical sun, and told him that the waters of the Indian Ocean were striped with beautiful shades of blue and green never seen in northern waters. She told him about the myriad gods of the Hindu religion, and the deep-rooted belief in peace and order that characterised Buddhism. And the terrible, inexplicable hatred that existed between the two faiths, arising from profound differences that had existed on the island since time immemorial.

She told him the names of all the good surfing beaches of the south-west: which ones were best for beginners, and which famous for waves that only an expert could master. And she told him, too, of the calm, sheltered harbours of the north-east, perfect for diving and for watching marine life. That gave him the opening he'd clearly been waiting for.

"You say you can't surf anymore."

She nodded grimly, but didn't argue. It was something she'd accepted, but she didn't have to pretend she liked it.

"What if you went back to a different part of Sri Lanka? Started up a whale-watching business, for instance? You'd still be at home, in your grandmother's part of the island, if I've understood you. As the financial partner you wouldn't need the physical strength that surfing once required. You could pay someone to deal with the practical side of things."

"Why are you saying this? I thought we'd decided I was

going to scatter Dad's ashes at sea and then come back. Don't you want me?"

"Not want you?" His hands went out to touch her, but she pulled away and glared at him. "Sushila, I will want you down all the years that are left to me, but you have to think about what's best for you."

"I want to be with you." The set of her mouth was stubborn. "I want to be here."

"Okay." He forbore to argue with her, but the next night, as they stood in the kitchen watching the rise of a swelling moon only a night or two from full, he started again.

"Sushila, you are so full of life. It's wonderful. It makes me love you more every time I see you. You shouldn't waste that life in an empty corner of the world. Think how much good you could do back on your own island. And you would come to love it again, I know you would."

She sulked and refused to look at him, but he persisted in trying to raise the unwelcome subject. At last she stormed out of the kitchen and ran into the bedroom, where she slammed the door in his face and refused to reply to his apology. She threw herself down on the bed and hid her face in the pillow. Out of the corner of her eye, she saw the gorgeous batik cloth lying crumpled on the floor and picked it up, smoothing it out between her fingers.

On some level she had to admit that he was right. The longer she spent with him, the stronger she felt, and the more capable she was of picking up the torn threads of her life and knitting them back into some kind of fulfilling and worthwhile whole. But she would just have to find a way of doing that here. She'd found something marvellous in this little corner of Scotland, and she was determined never to let it go. There must be some way to have it all.

With that realisation came a measure of forgiveness, and she opened the door and went back down to him. He stood when she came into the room, but didn't move towards her. She looked at his dear face and the long lines of him, and a powerful wave of desire washed through her. *How can I even think of leaving him?* She crossed the room and into his arms, and forgot everything in the warmth of his touch. That night she walked him to the door and watched him pull on his boots.

"Are you sure you won't stay?" she said, trying not to plead. He shook his head, pulled her to him and kissed her bruised lips again.

"Come to the spring tomorrow," he said. "Just before sunset. Wear something warm."

She slept like the dead that night, not waking until mid-morning, but the rest of the day was spent in frenetic non-activity as she fretted away the hours, trying to find tasks that would take her mind off the need to be with him. She took the bus into town and wandered up and down the main street, looking in all the windows, and wasting an hour or so over coffee and cake while she tried to focus her mind on the daily paper. The news of the world seemed overwhelmingly irrelevant.

On her second pass down the street she used a tourist's camera to take photos of his family with an enormous ginger tomcat that was lying in the middle of the road, apparently oblivious to passing traffic. It seemed he was some kind of local celebrity. People were queuing up to have their photos taken, and there were even ginger-cat postcards in the shops. Sushila bought some chocolate, feeling an obscure need for comfort food, but by the time the bus left she was well and truly ready to get home. She trudged up the track as quickly as her slightly achy leg would let her, shivering in the cool wind that was coming in from the north-west, and threw a few supplies into the pack, remembering to pull on her dad's old woollen bush-shirt, and stuff a hat into the side pocket.

The same cold wind followed her up the hill, and the fat, yellow rise of the moon began to light her way, as the sun went down behind the hill in a blaze of scarlet and magenta. Once again clouds were gathering, and this time they looked grey and heavy. Maybe Dougie was right and he would finally get his rain.

By the time she reached the spring the wind was blustery, and a few heavy drops of water had already fallen. The clouds were roiling in the sky, building with unbelievable speed. As she made her way around the side of the hill she was startled to spot patches of bog rush in the grass. Still no sign of moisture, but moisture-loving plants don't jump out of the ground overnight. Perhaps she was already back in Dougie's secret valley?

As she climbed down into the combe the moon was overtaken by the rushing cloud, and a wall of darkness blotted out the ground before her. She blinked, trying to see more clearly, and as her pupils adjusted she saw that she stood in a patch of boggy ground, and there were celandines dotting the grass at her feet. As she raised her head she saw him, and ran into his arms with a cry of gladness.

He didn't speak, but pulled the pack from her shoulders and dropped it, letting the walking poles fall beside it. He grasped her by the hand and pulled her with him, back the way she'd come and onto the summit of the hill. The moon flickered in and out of the clouds, and its fitful illumination made it seem that they were standing on an island in a sea of cloud and darkness.

She looked up at him happily and he grinned back, his teeth a white gleam in the dark as the moonlight caught the wild glint in his eye. She could feel a sense of tension building, like the excitement of a crowd watching a match, or the moment of stillness before a dam gives way. He reached down and lifted her so that her feet stood on top of his. He wrapped his fingers around her waist and held her. She leaned back in his grasp, totally trusting, and let her head hang back, hair flowing around his fingers as he began slowly to dance.

He laughed, and the sound was like thunder, and at that moment the heavens opened and the rain sluiced down, running over her face and soaking her hair. A bolt of lightning hit one of the trees on the edge of the hilltop and it exploded in flame, the fire immediately quenched by the force of the rain.

He began to spin, and she felt the movement of his feet as she rested on them, the centrifugal force starting to drive her upper body away from his. Bolt after bolt of lightning hit the turf around them, her body rung by the endless vibration passing through it, its energy fizzing in her nerve endings until she began to feel the power building from her feet up through the length of her spine, emerging like a column of light from the top of her head.

He laughed again, deep as the heart of the mountain, pulled her towards him and put his mouth down to hers. Their bodies merged in the darkness as the rain washed over them. Fully clothed, soaking wet, battered by the deluge, still he touched the core of her being, and she heard herself cry out as the feeling overwhelmed her and she clung to him, tears mingling with the rain.

She woke to find herself curled on a bed made from layers of animal skins, cloud-soft sheepskins and faded woollen plaids. Through an open doorway she could see the central hearth, and beyond it grey sky and falling sheets of rain. When she noticed she was wearing no clothes she rolled over and wrapped herself in a grey blanket whose faded shades seemed to mirror the weather outside. As she came to the inner doorway a man's shape crossed the light. Dougie ducked in the doorway, shaking droplets from his hair. He shivered, like a dog coming out of a river, and was instantly dry. He was also naked.

"Nice trick," she said, trying to lighten the moment as she averted her eyes.

"I expect you could do it, too, just at the moment," he replied.

There was no shame or embarrassment in his eyes, although he grinned in amusement at her discomfiture. The grin faltered as he continued to look at her, and a moment later he nodded and turned, pulling on his jeans from the pile of clothes on the floor. For some crazy reason, Sushila found herself accepting all the strange things that had happened, up to and including whatever it was that had filled her, body and soul, when she danced in this man's arms in the heart of a thunderstorm. But seeing him walk in out of the rain, clad in nothing but his own skin, was somehow frightening. It told her how far he had gone from human norms.

"Or maybe I've just stopped worrying about appearances," he said, taking the kettle from the hearth and pouring out two mugs of tea.

"Yeah, and that's another thing," she retorted, trying to hold onto the blanket with one hand while reaching out the other to take a mug from him. "Stop looking inside my head."

"Sorry." He looked unrepentant, and eyed her askance from under a mop of ragged curls.

"Your hair's grown," she said. It was at least two inches longer than it had been, and even curlier. It made him look like a fallen Botticelli angel.

He laughed. "So has yours."

She turned in a circle, trying to see the back of her own head. He was right. It felt heavier as it swirled about her. He stepped forward and took hold of it, running his fingers through it and tucking it back behind her ears. He reached behind her and opened a chest, taking out a small hairbrush. Its wooden handle was battered but it was scrupulously clean. He shunted her forward to the outer doorway, and she stood sipping her tea and gazing blindly into the curtain of rain, as he slowly and thoroughly brushed her hair. He worked until it fell like a single curtain of black silk from her crown straight down to her knees. Then he pulled her into him, nestling her back into his crotch, and, lifting her hair with both hands, kissed the side of her neck. She shivered and twisted, reaching for him, but he stepped back.

"I want to see you," he said.

She shook her head, avoiding his eyes.

"Sushila, you are beautiful. Please let me see you."

"Don't be daft. I am not beautiful. Don't forget, I'm Aby's daughter. I know what beauty really looks like. I was very ordinary compared to that. And that was before the leg."

She gestured loosely with the half-empty mug. She wasn't ashamed of her scars. Not anymore. They were just a part of her. But she was damned if she was going to parade them, especially in front of someone who already made her feel very vulnerable.

Dougie leaned against the wall and folded his arms. He frowned. "Aby was striking, I'll give you that. I can see why the camera loved her. Beauty is something else. It shines out from a person who possesses it. There's far more to it than simple physical attractiveness. You have it in abundance, but I tell you this, Sushila Priya Mackenzie: every inch of you attracts me. And the scars you bear on the inside cripple you far more effectively than what is left of the damage done to your leg."

Sushila bridled at the use of her full name—more rummaging inside her head—but then the import of his words struck home. *What is left?* She glanced down involuntarily and twitched the plaid aside to look at herself. Her leg still looked mangled and misshapen, but the rough, angry scars had faded to white, and the damaged muscle of her calf had rounded out a little. Now she became aware of a warm, slightly prickly feeling inside her leg, as if the accelerated process of healing was still going on.

She gasped and put her hands up to her mouth. With speed born of the lightning, Dougie leapt to her side and snatched away the blanket. Sushila was too surprised to stop him, and by the time she began to react he had caught her eyes in his own, and she found he was holding her calmly in place, without touching her at all. She jerked in surprise, feeling a wild need to escape, and he released her. She stayed where she was. With an effort of will she straightened her shoulders and stood, bare, before him. After all, he'd seen into the depths of her soul last night. What was there to fear in simple physical nakedness?

He put out one hand and cupped her cheek. "I couldn't undo all the damage," he said. "I can't put back what is gone. But I could speed up the healing process, move you years forward. You know, if you'd believed in yourself and persevered with the physiotherapy, you'd have done a lot of it for yourself over the last few years. So all I've done is bring you forward to the best you could be at this point. It will last, wherever you go. It's a permanent change."

As he spoke, he knelt at her feet, resting his head on her stomach, and ran his hands gently down her legs, smoothing the damaged left and the untouched right. His breath was cool on her skin and a shiver moved up her body. She felt herself tremble as it passed. His touch was deft and sure, and she felt safe under his hands.

"I expect this works quite well with horses, too," she joked.

"Never tried it," he said. "Works brilliantly with difficult ewes, though."

She snorted with laughter. "Compared to a sheep. That's me told."

He stood again and smiled down at her, holding out his hand. "Care to dance?"

She rested a hand on his shoulder, feeling the muscles there and at his waist sliding over one another as he moved her into the dance. He hummed a little under his breath and the sound of the water dripping from the eaves, and splashing into the puddles outside, blended with the tune into one melodic sound.

Gradually her breathing fell into sync with the music. Slowly he moved her around the hearth, stepping lightly on the earthen floor, and then, as the pace quickened, across the flagstone porch and out into the rain. Mist flowed into the hollow and covered her, like the lightest of silk scarves, and he lifted her again onto his feet. She closed her eyes and felt her heartbeat drumming in time with his as he whirled her away into the open, faster and faster, until two heartbeats blended into one and there was nothing left in the clearing but wind and rain.

She stepped down onto the grass again as easily as walking into her own front door, and as she ducked into the porch a mist poured away from her body and left her dry and bare. Dougie pulled the door closed behind them. He still wore the jeans he'd donned for her benefit, drying them with a wave of his hand, and she pulled on her own clothes, feeling more comfortable once conventionally dressed. She rested a hand on his upper arm as he sat down beside her.

"Will it always be like this?" she asked him.

"I can't be entirely sure," he told her. "It's never been like this before. But I don't think so. This is one of the high holidays of the year: first full moon after the spring equinox, and rain to die for after weeks of drought. Sooner or later things will settle down, but just at the moment I feel as though I could move mountains."

"I'm glad, I think. I couldn't live this way all the time. It's too much."

They sat for a while in companionable silence, but at length she stirred and Dougie looked down at her again. He put out a finger and smoothed the frown lines down the middle of her forehead. "Penny for your thoughts?"

The frown left her face and she smiled at him. "I was thinking. Do you feel anything from your wife? From Maire?"

"No." His face was sombre. "She didn't die on the mountain, and she's buried away in the churchyard. She didn't grow up here, either, so there's really nothing of her left. Apart from the bairn. He's here. But he never really lived, so I don't know anything about him."

"You know that he was a boy?"

"Yes, I suppose I do. He had nine months of life in Maire's womb. Enough to leave as much mark as a newborn lamb, landing on the hilltop. I do know he was definitely a boy. It still makes me sad that when they buried him he didn't even have a name."

"What were you going to call him?"

"I don't know. Maire said it was bad luck to name the bairn before it's born. She must have had her ideas, but she never told me." He looked at her gravely and reached out to take her hands in his. "Sushila, will you name my son?"

She bit her lip, her eyes shining. "I would be honoured to name him." She thought for a while, and then stirred again. "Dougie, would it be all right to name him Donald? After my father?"

He sighed, and tears gathered at the corners of his eyes. "It most certainly would."

They sat on for a moment, looking at each other, but she bent her head. A tear ran down her nose and dripped onto her thigh. He took her chin in his hand and turned her face back up to the light.

"And your baby?" he asked her.

"My baby was hardly more than a promise when I lost it. I never even found out whether it was a boy or a girl."

"Sushila, you know better than that. Look now; the secret is hidden within you. Your body knows."

She stared at him, her eyes big with tears, and slowly nodded. "Yes. I feel it. The child I lost was a boy. Alan's son."

"He knew, all along."

"Yes, he did, didn't he? Alan junior."

"And the Gaelic word *àlainn* means 'beautiful'."

Her head fell forward and she cried long and sweetly for the man and the child, swept away from her when their lives together had hardly begun. Dougie quietly stood and left her to mourn, knowing without words that she needed to be alone for a while. He moved about the house, putting things to rights, and went back into the rain to bring in another armful of wood for the fire. When the storm of weeping subsided he lifted her to her feet and kissed the tears from her face.

"Ready for something new?" he asked.

He towed her behind him to the back of the outhouse, where an overhanging roof kept the firewood and peats dry. Tucked away in a corner, lying on an old sack, was Flo, with four puppies. Still blind, they wriggled as they fed, looking like fat miniatures of their dam. The dog raised her head to look at them and her tail thumped on the ground.

"We're not the only ones to have experienced the benefits of last night's surge." He laughed at the look on her face.

"How on earth does a ghost dog get pregnant?"

"I have no idea, but it raises some interesting questions about you and me."

A grin spread across her face. "Yes, I'd say it does."

He held out his hand and she took it, gripping it between both of hers, as a wild surmise flew across her mind. She fought it down, tucking it away in some buried pocket of her subconscious. Something to think about later. Much later.

"Shall we dance?"

"Never mind dancing," she said, pulling him to her. "What about dinner? You may not need it, but I haven't eaten for hours."

1909

The fence creaked as each man climbed it. In the clear night air, their voices carried, and he could see the intermittent glow of the cigarette that was permanently tucked into Lachlan's lip. His brother brought up the rear, carrying the pouch of ammunition, but it was Lachlan who bore the gun.

The boy waited until all sound of their passing died away, then climbed the fence carefully at the strainer post. His light weight hardly stressed it, but he felt the vibration of his movement transmitted down the wire. He clutched his plaid around himself, feeling the night chill working its way under his clothes, and followed.

Initially, the men made no attempt to be quiet, laughing and joking as they climbed the hill. Soon enough, though, they turned and made their way across the hill flank towards the dark woods. Gradually the talk died away as they began to mentally prepare themselves for the stalking. The waning moon rose and laid its buttery light over the land. The men were quiet now, moving shadows, and the boy crouched in a hollow and watched them, not daring to get too close.

At the wood's edge, Lachlan dropped his cigarette and ground it out on the turf. Just before they entered the trees, the second man in line turned and looked behind him. The boy froze, convinced he'd been seen, but the man turned back without a sound and disappeared under the eaves of the small wood. Dougie allowed himself to breathe again. He was frightened of Iain Gowan. The smith was a big man with small tolerance for children. Never mind that, at fifteen, Dougie didn't believe he should be treated as a child anymore; he still wouldn't willingly cross Iain Gowan.

Especially on a hunt, after he'd been expressly refused permission to follow.

Stalking the stalkers became more difficult when he entered the wood. It was difficult to see anything clearly in the confusing half-light cast by the moon, and even harder to avoid making a noise. The experienced hunters ahead of him were as silent as shadows in the darkness, although one did curse briefly under his voice when he tripped over a tree root. Dougie was pretty sure it was Donald. His brother, at eighteen, had only been on a handful of hunts before.

Something warned him. Some inchoate sense of what was ahead, for he could see nothing but shadows, and all was silent and still. The boy stopped on the edge of a clearing. Before him stood a young stag, no more than six points on its antlers, proud in the silence. The animal stood motionless, its head raised, not yet aware of its danger. To his left, the boy was vaguely aware that a figure crouched, aiming the gun, but all his attention was focused on the beautiful thing that stood before him. The boy drew a breath in wonder.

At the sound, faint but unmistakably human, the stag whirled and crashed away through the undergrowth. Lachlan threw down the gun and cursed. From out of the darkness, Donald appeared and dragged his brother forward into the clearing.

"Here he is. I told you he would follow us."

Lachlan grunted, amused. "Did you so, *a ghillean*? And did you not feel his sign, thrumming down the fence wires, and his heavy tread over the ground? Did you not see his shadow, flitting between hollows, back there on the hillside? Call yourself a hunter?"

Dougie struggled to get free of Donald's painful grip on his arm. Dropping his head, he bit his brother, who dropped him, swearing. Dougie turned to run, but collided instead with the heavy body of the smith, who put out one massive arm to stop him. He crouched, panting, in the midst of the men.

"What are we to do with the wee *piseag, a charaid?*" Iain Gowan asked.

Dougie bridled at the insult, but subsided under the smith's stern glance.

"Deal with him," Lachlan told his brother. "This is not a game for children. Make him remember it."

The older men gathered themselves and moved into the darkness, making no more sound than the quarry they sought. Donald held him again; Dougie could feel him shaking with fury and humiliation. He'd fought hard for his place among the hunters, and now his younger brother had come along to ruin everything. He wasted no words, simply drew back his fist and aimed it at Dougie's face.

He couldn't have been knocked out for more than a moment; he could still hear his brother's passage through the undergrowth. Dougie cradled his aching jaw, moving it from side to side and checking that he still had all his teeth. Then he crept forward, following the faint sounds of Donald's passage.

This time he took the deer's way, as wary of the men as he was of the wild things. Even the experienced ears of Lachlan MacEachan could not have distinguished his movements from the night sounds of the wood. He came upon the men again, a scant hour later, near the farther edge of the trees. A young stag, possibly the same one, had halted on the very edge of the foliage. It was content and unaware, quietly cropping leaves from the canopy, silhouetted by the moon.

The boy held his breath, not daring to move, while Lachlan took the shot, calmly squeezing the trigger and making a clean kill. Dougie crouched on, stiffening but determined to remain still. As the men moved forward and began to gut the carcass, Lachlan cleaned the gun and slung it onto his back. Then he turned and strode into the wood. He grasped Dougie by the hair and pulled him forward.

"Here's another who was in at the kill," he said, shaking

the slight figure of the boy. "What are we to do here?"

Iain Gowan looked up from his task. A brief grin crossed his face.

"You have the ears of a cat yourself, *a charaid*. I did not know he was still following."

Lachlan grasped Dougie's jaw and turned it into the moonlight, examining the bruise that was spreading there. "You took a man's blow, lad, and made no sound. You'll do for me."

While Dougie was still assimilating this cryptic comment, the smith rose from the carcass, a handful of guts in his hand. Taking Dougie by the shoulder, he rubbed the stinking offal over his head. Dougie stood, the bloodied mess dripping down his face, as the smith turned away.

"Come here, lad," the big man said. "There's an art to the gralloching. It's time you learned it."

12

☽ NARWHAL ☾

It rained without stopping for three days. On the fourth evening Dougie pulled her out of the house and back up onto the hill. There they danced again as another thunderstorm shook the landscape, but already Sushila could feel that the power was subsiding from its almost unbearable peak. The ground was sodden with water and still charged with energy. The spring exploded out of its alcove with palpable force, carving out a straighter path down the hill towards her house.

Even when she wasn't touching Dougie she felt light and ethereal, as if the wind could lift her, or, perhaps, simply pass through her and move on. She wanted to stay in that other-worldly state forever, suspended in time, free from the constraints and demands of reality, but she knew before he spoke what he was going to say.

"*Feumaidh thu falbh, m'eudail.* You must go, darling. It's time you took back your life."

It hurt to walk down the hill. Not her legs: both had continued to strengthen and the injured one now looked little different to the other. It hurt to turn her back on him, even for a moment, and let him go. She told herself not to cling, that it was only for a short time. It still hurt, though.

The house was musty and empty-smelling. It felt as though she'd been away for four months rather than four days. She walked down the track towards the road and turned on her phone to confirm it: four days only, though a lifetime away from her old life. She tried to turn her mind to mundane matters (shopping, cleaning, planning the journey that lay ahead) but her mind kept drifting back to that rain-battered hilltop and the man who had claimed her, body and soul.

Already the events of the last ten years had retreated in her mind: still there, still distressing but no longer immediate. Once again, she could feel the powerful, abiding love she and Alan had once shared. No longer blocked from her by a few moments of terrible trauma and a decade of unassuaged grief, now his memory was a comforting part of her distant past.

Humming absently, Sushila meandered along the road and surprised herself by arriving at the outskirts of the town. The bus overtook her as she walked down the hill. It wasn't that far, after all. She pulled herself together as she hit the main street. It wouldn't do to be daydreaming as she made her way through the growing tourist traffic. She smiled back at those locals who caught her eye, and realised that she enjoyed the feeling of being recognised, of belonging.

After an hour or so of half-hearted shopping her backpack was already full and she was thinking more clearly about everything she needed to do. Turning on her heel at the far end of the main street, she headed back to the garage at the bottom of the hill, taking action on an idea that had just popped into her head. The waves of tourists parted and she saw ahead of her a cabled jersey and a long pair of jeans thrust into worn work boots. She was opening her mouth to call him when he turned and crossed the street to the door of the pub. It was recognisably the same man who had hoisted her case on the ferry and carried it upstairs for her. But it was not Dougie. This man was older, with brown hair and eyes; the same weathered outdoors face, but with broken veins on his cheeks from exposure to the elements, or perhaps from drinking. He greeted the smokers at the door and ducked into the pub.

She was disconcerted for a moment but shook it off. So the man she'd met so briefly on the ferry had not been her ghostly partner, but a flesh and blood man. There was definitely a resemblance, though, and it led her to wonder if Dougie had living relatives. That was a strange thought to ponder. If a living woman could, like a ghost dog, bear the offspring of the little god of the spring, would those children be relatives of Dougie's living family? Or would there be no kinship at all? In fact, would such a child even be human? Or would it be tied to Dougie's existence on the hill, and not able to interact with the human world at all? These were lonely and disconcerting thoughts, and Sushila didn't want to have them. Besides, it was much too early to be thinking such things. She couldn't imagine raising such an issue with Dougie. Not yet, anyway.

She ducked into the garage and had a word with the owner. Yes, there was a car available to hire. It was being serviced, but he could have it for her by six p.m. if she cared to wait, or she could collect it in the morning. She agreed to pick it up at six and shouldered her pack again for the brief walk to a nearby coffee shop. She sat there, nursing a cappuccino, and wrote out a long list of tasks and a slightly shorter list of purchases.

By the time six o'clock arrived she was laden with bags and parcels, which she gratefully decanted into the boot of the small car. The garage owner handed over the keys and she paid for a week's hire, with the option to keep the car for a further week if she needed it. After a quick detour to collect some bags she'd left on the pavement outside the supermarket, Sushila headed home. When she pulled up outside the house she was surprised to see lights in the window.

The porch was swept and clean, the hallway floor gleamed and the windows were freshly polished. As she opened the door into the living room a sharp smell of soot ambushed her nostrils and she sneezed loudly. Dougie was on his hands and knees, sweeping. The rest of the room was clean and kindling was laid out on the grate, ready to light, but the hearthrug looked as though it was probably beyond redeeming. It would certainly never be white again.

A chagrined face looked up at hers, then he clambered to his feet.

"I was trying to be clever. Thought you'd like a fire tonight, but the chimney was blocked."

"Dad only came here in the summer. I don't think that fire's been used for decades."

"Yes, well, probably you're right. Anyway, I called a wind to clear the blockage, but it was stronger than I expected."

Sushila laughed. Tears welled up and took her completely by surprise. She laughed until they ran from her eyes and he laughed with her, until he gathered her up in his arms and turned the joy into kissing. She wiped her eyes and took a breath, still feeling the laugh in the base of her throat.

"I wish I'd been here to see it."

"I don't." His tone was rueful. "You should have seen the room before I cleaned it. Sorry about the rug. I'm not sure what to do with it now."

"Throw it out. It's been there for years. I'm pretty sure it was more grey than white anyway."

"Well, now it's ruined. I wish I could say I'd go out and buy you another one. But I can't go out. And anyway I don't know what I'd use for money. I seem to be remembering quite a few things that I used to do before, and don't bother with now."

Sushila led the way to the kitchen and unloaded a double armful of parcels. She filled a pot with water and started to prepare pasta and sauce. She cut chunks of baguette and Dougie buttered them, and a few minutes later they sat down together at the kitchen table and ate. The feeling of food sliding down her gullet grounded her and she began to feel more human again. Dougie ate too, but slowly, not needing the sustenance, and he watched her as he ate. After a while he nodded and sat back in his chair, tipping it backwards to press the button on the kettle to start it boiling.

"My dad told me off for doing that," Sushila remarked, her mouth still full of bread. "He used to threaten to tip me onto the floor."

"Gran said the same to me." Their eyes met as he shared the joke. "I guess kids have been doing it as long as there have been chairs."

"Dougie, I've been thinking. You say you are bound to your hill. You can come here, I guess, because the spring runs past the door and into the plumbing. You said there was a wee shop on the other side of the hill, but have you been there since, you know—since you became what you are?"

"Yes, I still go once in a blue moon. Whenever I need something I can't manufacture for myself, or just sometimes when I need some human company. "

"How often is once in a blue moon?"

"I haven't done it for about ten years. Don't even know if the shop's still there, actually."

"What did you use for money then, if you don't mind me asking?"

"Fairy gold."

"Pfft." Sushila was dismissive. "No, I'm being serious."

"So am I. I always seemed to have enough in my pocket, and no-one ever said the next time that my money hadn't been good, or had melted away after I'd left."

"Not fairy gold then. I've always read that fairy gold turns back into dust or dead leaves when the glamour is off it. This sounds more as though you can manufacture whatever you need, 'need' being defined by whatever makes you happy at the time. That makes me wonder something else, though. Why do you need me? Surely you can conjure up a woman out of your own desires, and she'd be perfect because she'd be based purely on what you want and need?"

Dougie stared at her, a hurt expression on his face, but he relaxed after a moment and sighed. "The fact you can even think it tells me you don't understand how much you mean to me. I suspect Flo and her puppies do arise out of my need for company, for all that she seems to have a will of her own, but the last thing I've ever wanted is a puppet woman, constructed to meet my every desire but without a thought in her head that I didn't put there."

"I'd have thought that was every man's dream."

"Then you don't know much about men."

Sushila pulled herself to her feet to put the dirty dishes in the sink, and busied herself making tea. "I can't argue with that," she said.

Dougie grabbed her arm and pulled her down into his lap. She held his face between her hands and gazed at him, wondering at the feelings that welled up inside her at the sight of this man.

"Would it surprise you to know that I'd never thought of such a thing? That in all my years on the hill, lonely or not, I never thought to create a companion? It took you, *mo leannan*, to break my sleep and show me that ghost, spirit or whatever I may be, I still have physical and emotional needs. And that, my love, is the power you have over me."

This time his lips were soft on hers, his arms enfolding her as she ran her fingers through his hair and across his back. Rising, he lifted her and carried her through to the bedroom. Her hands shook as she pulled open his shirt and opened the fly of his jeans.

As they fell to his feet she caught sight of his reflection in the mirror behind him. "I didn't know you had a tattoo," she said.

Half turning, he examined himself in the mirror. Across the right side of his back, mirroring the curve of the top of his buttock, a blue, spiralled shape marked his skin. Dougie admired himself, with an air of fascination. "I've never seen it myself," he said. "I mean, I remember getting it, but I've never seen it in a mirror before."

"It looks like a dolphin," she said. "Leaping from the water. I can see the surface of the water in front of it—that line. No, it isn't water. I think it's more like…"

"It's a horn," he said. "A narwhal. The mark of my clan."

She watched her hand in the mirror as it traced the shape of the sea-beast with its astonishing horn, and followed with her finger the spirals and coils of blue that filled the tattoo.

"I think there were meant to be more," he said. "But I only got the first one. That's the only one that's really needed, though." Shrugging off this enigmatic remark, he bent his head and laid his lips gently on hers, kissing her softly, and then with greater need.

Stepping out of the pile of clothes on the floor, he turned his attention to her body, stripping her clothes with methodical care and laying them aside. She felt a pang of shyness, but it was lost in the warmth of his kiss, the delicious sensation of his hands exploring her body, his tongue on her ear, her hand on his flank, fingers and feet, mouths and tangled limbs. An endless moment of delight when it became impossible to tell who was touching whom, or where, and the feeling rose to a dizzying ecstasy that swept them both away.

1914

Dougie lay on his stomach, sucking in steady breaths against the pain. His right buttock ached, and a hot wire ran under his skin and up the curve of his spine. He tried not to move.

The door opened, its movement sending a cold draught across his back. His skin shivered and Dougie bit back a cry. The burning sensation seemed to be growing. He was sure it hurt more now than when his grandmother had applied the needles. That had been agony, though: an endless, confusing red wave of pain, in the midst of which he had fallen into some very strange dreams.

Donald crossed the floor and crouched at the bedside, so that Dougie could see his face. His brother's expression was the usual combination of reluctant sympathy and irritated confusion.

"So, you went through with it, then."

"It would seem so."

"I thought you were going to come with me."

Dougie held his brother's eyes for a moment, but didn't answer.

"They say there's going to be a war. I've already got my posting, in the merchant navy, but if you wait they might take you for the regiment. You won't have any choice."

Dougie shook his head slightly, his face brushing against the rough wool of his spread plaid. "They won't take me," he said.

"You don't know that. If you come with me I'll put in a word. We might even crew on the same vessel. It's a good life."

"My life is here. It's what I've chosen."

A frown creasing his face, his brother strove to understand. "It's that thing with Gran, isn't it? I don't understand it. Is that why you decided to get the tattoo?"

"Yes, that's part of it."

"You talk like it's some kind of weird mystery, when it's nothing but superstition. All that nonsense about the life of water and air and fire, it's all mumbo jumbo. Worse than the bloody church. How can you believe that stuff?"

"It's right for me. That's all I know."

Donald gave in, sinking to the earthen floor and hugging his knees. "I've never understood you," he said.

Dougie made no reply to this self-evident remark. He gazed at Donald, memorising his face. It was going to be a long time before they saw each other again.

"I'm going to miss you," he said.

"Yeah, maybe—like a dog misses a horsefly."

"Ha!" Dougie's laugh shook his frame, and the pain flared again, but he ignored it. "You said it, *a dhuine*."

Donald stood and ruffled his brother's hair affectionately. Dougie tolerated it, but spoke as Donald turned away.

"What about Eilidh MacDonald?"

"She knows I'm away to sea. She's not happy, but she'll thole it."

"She's carrying your baby."

"She is not! Anyway, we only did it twice." Donald stood stock still in the middle of the room, glaring down at the figure on the bed. "How in hell did you know about that?"

"I felt it."

"Oh, not that again. You do not 'feel' other people's conditions. If you think you feel Eilidh MacDonald, you're welcome to her. If she slept with me, she'll sleep with second-best when she starts to feel the need. And she isn't pregnant."

"Suit yourself. When the time comes, I'll look after her."

"You do that." Donald slammed out of the room, and Dougie heard the noise of his passage through the front of the house. He sank his awareness deep into the hill and sensed his brother's angry strides down the valley. He was taking the long way round to the town—past Eilidh's door. Dougie smiled to himself. He wondered what the child would look like.

He shifted uncomfortably; the blood had dried and the inked skin had stiffened. He thought back to the ritual his grandmother had performed, as she laid each pinprick into his skin and ground in the mixture of ash and burned stone that would give his tattoo its blue colouring. She, too, bore the leaping narwhal on her back, and other designs, hidden under her clothing and the fall of her hair. Not as many, though, as Grandfather.

Dougie had known the blue man all his life. The tattooed figure appeared in his dreams, often imparting useful information or smoothing the way to some troubling realisation. The boy had felt the old man's presence at his shoulder, unseen, at some of the most difficult moments of his life. But it was only through the ritual that he'd gradually become aware that his grandmother, too, knew the blue man. That she, and he, were part of a line of awareness that had belonged to this land, this place and its waters, from the time that the great ocean opened, the molten land cooled and the first water arose in its spring.

This morning she had fed him bitter-tasting foods, and a strong drink of whisky and herbs, laid him down on this bed, and sung to him until he entered a strange time of lights and visions. All the time she worked she sang: a half-droning chant at the edge of hearing in a language he didn't understand.

The tattoo, and the slow process of its making, brought together all the pinprick moments of awareness. At the zenith of his agony he completely understood the power of his lineage and even the language of her song became clear to him. Now, though, it was all about the ache in his back and the dark confusion in his mind. He tried to hold to the understanding he'd reached but it was receding, like the aftermath of broken sleep.

The brief draught came again as his grandmother entered the room, carrying a pottery mug filled with a soothing drink. She helped him turn onto his side and drink it, before settling him down again and laying her hand on his hair.

"I had the strangest dream," he said, as the herbs in the drink took away his pain and he began to slide back into the dark.

"I expect you did, *a ghràidh*."

13
☽ FAIRY GOLD ☾

Their first boundary-testing experiment was a qualified success. After a fortifying visit to the still, where Dougie refilled his hip flask and took a long draught of the pure spring water, he led the way around the side of the hill and down its northern flank, past another scatter of tumbled foundations and the remains of a fank that looked to be in better repair than any of the ruined dwellings. Still, there was no sign that it had held sheep in recent times.

Dougie passed it without a word and Sushila was content to follow. The sun was out and the air steamed as every blade of grass transpired its moisture back into the atmosphere. Now that the ground was supersaturated and the spring in full spate, Dougie seemed unconcerned about the clear blue sky and sunshine. She pondered whether, like the plants he was striding through, he could draw the moisture up from the deep earth all the way to the crown of his head. He turned and caught her gazing at him.

"What?"

"I was wondering if I was going to see steam escaping from your ears."

He laughed and strode back to her, hauling her off her feet and kissing her soundly. She staggered a little when he set her down and followed him as docilely as a pet ewe when he turned and walked on. There was still residual stiffness from their activities last night, and she enjoyed the unaccustomed stretch and ache in parts of her body that had not been used for a very long time. She basked in the memory and became conscious that she was smiling. She deliberately relaxed her facial muscles, but as soon as she stopped being aware of it the smile returned.

The little shop was still there. Perhaps fortunately, its current proprietor was not known to Dougie and he ducked inside without qualm. Once in, however, he seemed disconcerted. Sushila tried to imagine what might be worrying him. Surely, products hadn't changed that much in a decade?

"Are you sure you were here ten years ago?" she murmured in his ear.

He shuffled his feet. "It might have been more like thirty. What *is* all this stuff?"

In the end he bought some potatoes, flour and yeast, dried fruit and some fresh, crisp apples which they ate on their way back up the hill. Sushila found it interesting that he showed no interest in any kind of processed food, buying only raw ingredients that he could turn into recipes at home. She wondered if that was habit, or perhaps it was necessary that at some level everything he ate had to involve contact with water from the spring. He had no need to borrow any money from her. Just as he'd said, he put his hand in his pocket and the right money was there, barring a few coppers in change that now jingled as he walked.

Back at his house there was fresh bread rising and water to be drawn from the barrel. While the bread baked, Sushila took a walk around the back of the house to visit Flo in her den. She bent down and called softly, and the dog emerged. This time she was accompanied by only one puppy, and this one half grown. It hardly seemed possible it had grown so much in only a few days. More magic at work, she thought, as she fondled it and stroked Flo. The two of them followed her back to the porch and she met Dougie coming out. He whistled Flo to his side and patted her absently, his eyes following the puppy.

"I suppose she only needed the one," he said. Sushila caught his eye and he shrugged. "I don't know," he said, in answer to her unspoken question. "She gave birth to four, but now there's only one. This must be what she needs. It'll not be long and I can start to train him. But she keeps him in order now."

The puppy barked at this, sat down and started scratching. Sushila grinned. "Do ghost dogs have ghost fleas?"

"Oh yes. But only enough to allow for some pleasurable scratching. And Flo's never had a tick. That's one thing I don't miss."

Fresh bread and cool water, an afternoon of lovemaking and an evening of drowsy chat. It was one of those timeless days that seem to last forever, and yet are over all too soon. They slept on the hill that night, wrapped up in blankets as the stars wheeled overhead, and she pillowed her head on his chest and listened to his heartbeat, the low rumble of his voice following her into sleep just as dawn began to break. She woke to dew in her hair.

They spread the blankets out to air and headed down to the white cottage. It didn't feel quite so empty and unloved now that it held the memory of lovemaking, but Sushila noted the weeds pushing their way up around the edges of the yard. It wouldn't take much neglect for her absence to become obvious. She didn't want the community to realise she was staying away, and her recent visit to the town with its friendly (and nosy) local community had made her aware that even though the cottage felt isolated, local folk were very well aware of who was living there, and probably had a good idea of her movements. If anyone found it strange that she was spending nights on the hill, they hadn't said anything yet, but it was probably only a matter of time.

Did it really matter if people knew? After all, if things went according to plan Dougie ought to be able to allow himself to be seen by others, and they could pretend they were normal people with a normal relationship. She shied away from examining why it mattered to her what people thought.

Today's experiment involved a bit more than a walk down the hill and retail therapy. Dougie fortified himself with a quick swig from the kitchen tap while Sushila packed a few picnic essentials. Then she opened the car doors and wound down the windows, letting the hot air out. Dougie loped out into the yard, closing the door behind him, and climbed into the passenger seat. He quickly figured out how the seat belt worked. Today, he was wearing an old-fashioned button-collared cotton shirt, rather worn and with the sleeves rolled up, and a pair of decidedly late-twentieth century jeans. He looked perfectly at home in the car, and no-one seeing the pair of them driving along would think they were any different to a normal couple.

He shut the passenger door as Sushila climbed in behind the wheel. She turned to speak to him as she pulled the driver's door shut. With the faintest of almost-imaginary hisses, his form dissolved. One moment he was there. The next: gone. Sushila reached across and groped at the passenger seat. Her hand struck the back of the seat and she found herself patting its cushion and choking back tears. This was not what she'd planned!

She opened the door and jumped out of the car, feeling sick and dizzy. For a moment she stood with her head hanging, then straightened and looked round at the car. His face was there, his body slumped into the seat and a look of bemusement on his face. Sushila pulled open the passenger door and almost fell on top of him. He pulled her onto his lap and wrapped his arms around her, seeing her obvious distress.

"What happened? I was all ready to go and you turned white as a sheet and jumped out of the car. What upset you?"

"You were gone." She was still almost incoherent. "I looked across and you were just gone. I thought I'd lost you."

Pushing her out of the car, he took off the seatbelt and unfolded himself, gathering her into his embrace and pulling her tight to him. He rested his chin on her head and stroked her back, calming her.

"I was still there. It's an interesting thing that happened, but don't worry. I was definitely still there."

Sushila pulled herself together. She hadn't lost him; there was no point in over-reacting to what had occurred. Now she was becoming interested in the mechanics of the situation.

"You were there right up to the point that I closed my door. When I jumped out, I suppose you reappeared, but I was so upset I didn't notice. It's as if closing the door shuts you off from the environment. That doesn't happen inside the house."

"Well, you can view the house as a single entity with the spring water running right through the plumbing. The car is different. It's a separate environment from the outside, and there's no spring water here but what's in my little flask."

Sushila pulled herself out of his embrace. "I have an idea." She ran into the kitchen and grabbed one of the empty water containers, filling it from the ample supply now running from the tap. She opened up the bonnet and checked the car's water levels. There was room to add more, and she poured almost half a litre into the coolant reserve and topped up the windscreen washers for good measure. Dumping the container next to the porch she went back to the car.

"Shall we try again?"

It made no difference. For whatever reason, the car was different to the house. As soon as all the doors were closed, Dougie disappeared. He claimed he was still there, and after a couple more heart-stopping moments she began to accept it. She wanted to stop the experiment there. They couldn't use the car, it was too dangerous. It wasn't worth the risk. Dougie was sanguine.

"Drive round the corner, down to the MacDougalls' letterbox. I've walked that far before now. When you get back, we'll see."

And it worked. Back on the yard Sushila opened the door and there he was. Maddeningly, it seemed that he could travel incognito for a small distance, but she wasn't going to be able to drive proudly with him at her side. Sushila stalked into the house and made two mugs of tea. She wouldn't admit to herself that she'd been looking forward to being seen with him. She'd allowed herself to see the future: going about her business with the good looking man at her side, showing off her good fortune to the world.

She handed him his mug and controlled her temper with an effort. So much good had happened to her since they'd met. She couldn't blame him for his failure to meet what were probably quite unrealistic expectations. She blamed herself for having them in the first place. Dougie, as usual, seemed to be fully aware of her feelings, just when she would really like to have hidden them. Bad enough to feel she'd humiliated herself without him realising it.

Sushila mentally chided herself and Dougie grinned at her, almost as if he'd heard the thought. She winced. They were drinking tea made from the spring water and they'd been arm-in-arm and soaked in each other's bodily fluids a few hours before. She huffed in exasperation. Probably he'd heard exactly what she was thinking.

He put down his tea and nuzzled her hair, reaching to take her mug and thump it down on the bench. He lifted her slightly and sat her on the kitchen table, kneeling between her legs so that he was looking up at her. She regarded his honest, earnest face and relented. "I love you," she said, rather surprising herself. He continued to look up at her.

"I know," he said, ducking his head to rub his nose into her crotch. She felt a spike of arousal shoot through her and grabbed his hair, hauling him upwards as she pulled herself into him. He kissed her thoughtfully, then put her away from him and looked at her again.

"I can't be everything you want me to be. But I will be everything I can to you. That's a promise I can keep, and you can believe in. And some of the time I know what you're thinking because I'm thinking the same thing myself. I would never willingly humiliate you. I hope you know that."

She nodded, feeling terrible, but he grabbed her hand and pulled her outside again.

"Come on, we're going to try again."

"What? No! No, I don't want to risk losing you."

"Sushila Mackenzie, look at me."

She stared up into his face, memorising every pore of it. If he was going to disappear in her car she was not going to forget him. Never.

"I am not going to disappear in your car. You are going to get in and drive at least five miles away from my hill. Park in a place where we're not overlooked. Then we'll see what we shall see."

He climbed into the passenger seat, fastened the seatbelt and pulled the door closed. At once he disappeared. Sushila walked round to the driver's side, her eyes pricking with unshed tears, and opened the door. She took the wheel in both hands, gripping it tightly, before turning to look in his eyes. She held them with hers as she reached one hand blindly for her own door and slammed it shut. He was gone in the moment that the lock clicked into place.

Fighting back the tears, she put the car into gear and pulled out over the cattle grid. The car bumped down the track and turned onto the main road, heading away from town. After six miles she pulled into a grassy track that led into an unkempt forestry block, and pulled the car to a halt under the spindly branches of a larch. She sighed, reached out her hand again, and opened the car door.

Dougie's kind, worn, dear face popped into view like a rabbit from a hat. Despite preparing herself, Sushila jumped and squealed. His laugh, rich and glorious, filled the car. He pulled her towards him and kissed her on the nose. "Worrywart," he said affectionately.

The next few days flew by, the two of them trotting

backwards and forwards between their two houses, equally at home in either, but gradually the balance shifted towards Dougie's house. One day he taught her to make bread, standing behind her as she kneaded the dough, her body pressed against his, Dougie's warm hands over hers as she shaped the bread. She leaned back into the heat of his torso and laughed from deep in her belly.

"Are you sure you haven't watched any films in the last, oh, forty years or so?"

"Quite sure. Why?"

"Oh, nothing."

1953

Dragging the sack onto his shoulders, the old man hauled himself to his feet and began to trudge uphill again. He flicked his eyes upwards along the line of the slope. There. He'd reach that next boulder. Then he could sit down again if he needed to.

Not for the first time, he cursed his failing body. Every time he went to town for supplies it seemed to become harder to climb the hill. Wheezing, he forced himself to put one foot in front of the other. His traitorous heart skipped a beat or two and he felt his vision darken. Groping before himself, he felt the surface of the boulder and sank down onto it. He had enough presence of mind to lay the sack down carefully before his knees gave out. The last thing he wanted was to be chasing downhill after a can of oil or a bag of dried peas that had tumbled out of the sack and away.

He rubbed his hand over his eyes to clear them and gazed out across the valley. The day was warm and bright, but the valley was filled with a mass of cloud. He tried to make out the stones of the small graveyard where his wife and child were buried, but could see nothing through the haze. Or perhaps the haziness was in his own eyes? It was hard to tell, these days.

Above him, on the hillside, a lark raised its voice in song. The beauty of it stirred the old man and his eyes filled with tears. He shook his head at the bird, or perhaps at someone beyond the range of sight, away up there on the hilltop.

"I hear ye, old woman," he muttered. "I'm coming."

Struggling to his feet, he began the journey again.

14
☽ A CAT MAY LOOK ☾

They were in the garden when the car pulled up, Sushila down on her hands and knees pulling weeds out of the bed beside the front door and Dougie leaning on the wall of the porch, taking a breather from weeding the bed on the other side. Sushila stood and rubbed her hands down the legs of her jeans, then walked round to the driver's side where Mary was rolling down the window. Looking in, she saw an elderly man sitting in the passenger seating, looking rather grey in the face and tired, and Morgan squashed into the back with a disreputable looking collie.

"Dad's had a bad turn and we're taking him down to the hospital. I've called and they're going to admit him for some respite care, so I'm taking the dog home with me, but we had to leave the cat behind. It lives outside mostly so it'll probably be fine. I wondered if you would mind feeding it and keeping an eye on it? It's the wee brown house opposite the MacDougalls' turnoff, just up the road there."

Sushila nodded. "Of course I will. What's the cat's name?"

"Mittens, but she answers just as happily to 'Hey you'. Morgan, would you give Sue the food?"

Morgan opened the back door and swung out a heavy carrier bag full of tins and a bag of dried food.

"Please keep an eye on her water supply. She gets it from the dripping tap out the back, but if the water gets cut off for any reason she'll need a bowl put out. Otherwise you shouldn't need to worry about her."

Sushila lifted her hand to wave as the little car reversed smartly and set off back down the track. She picked up the bag of cat food and tucked it in to a corner of the porch. She looked at Dougie who was still leaning on the door post, picking the dirt out from under his nails with his pocket knife.

"I can't believe Mary resisted the urge to say something, after all their teasing about me needing a man. It's like they didn't even notice you," she said.

"They didn't see me."

"How could they not see you? You were standing there the whole time." Then she realised what he was saying. "Oh, Dougie. Are you telling me I'm the only person who can see you?"

He nodded. "It may be. I wasn't sure the lady in the shop could really see me the other day. I think she noticed you talking to me, and of course I wanted to buy something, so her mind filled in the gaps. I didn't tell you beforehand, because I didn't want to upset you, but the last time I tried to enter the shop they couldn't see or hear me at all. I'd be willing to bet that if you went back there today and asked her, she wouldn't remember me.

"Your friends needed to talk to you. There was no need for them to be aware of me. So they weren't. I'm pretty sure you are the only person on the planet who is aware of me all the time."

"We'll never be able to be openly together if no-one else can see you. They'll all think I'm mad, talking to the air, or something."

"Does that matter?"

She stared at him, thinking of all the occasions on which she might need to have her partner by her side. Being with Dougie was so simple now that they understood one another; it was frighteningly easy to forget that he was not like other men. She struggled to explain why it mattered for them to be able to live normally among other human beings. She couldn't find the words, but he met her eyes with sombre acknowledgement and she realised he already understood.

Later that day they walked up to the little house on the corner to feed the cat. Sushila's feet scuffed along the gravel road and a light breeze fingered her hair as they walked, Dougie swinging the bag of cat food from one hand as he sauntered beside her. She shoved her hands into her pockets, and he slid his free hand in as well, to intertwine his fingers with hers. She reflected that anyone passing by would see only a woman walking by herself. Or would they see a bag of cat food hanging in the air? She giggled.

At that moment, the bin lorry rumbled its way past and ground to a halt outside the MacDougalls' house. Two men jumped down and collected the bins outside both houses, and Sushila concentrated on looking like a woman who was happily unaccompanied and definitely not talking to herself. Dougie's hand tightened on hers, but he didn't speak. She watched the lorry's dust trail depart round the corner and sighed. This invisible boyfriend business was going to cause problems.

The response of Mary's father's cat gave her more food for thought. It watched them from under the enormous cotoneaster that was taking over the path to the house. The shrub, with its tiny pink flowers, was alive with bees and the cat crouched beneath it, unwinking eyes fixed firmly on the interlopers. Sushila stayed away from it, not sure whether it was friendly, but Dougie sat down cross-legged on the path and talked to it, looking away into the garden with his hand laid down on the path near the frightened animal. By the time she had finished spooning out the food and checking there was water, the cat had slunk out from her hiding place and was winding herself around Dougie's arm, rubbing her head against his palm and purring.

"She can see you."

Dougie shrugged. He didn't seem surprised.

Sushila had a sudden thought. "Is Flo a real dog?"

"She's as real as you or me."

Sushila grunted in frustration. "You know what I mean."

"I do," he paused. "I'm sorry not to be clearer. You are as real to me as this lovely girl," he scratched under the cat's chin and the volume of her purring increased, "but most people are not real to me at all. To put myself in your shoes, I don't think Flo is a living animal, not like the cat here. She has been with me for a very long time, and she has never aged, so I think she can't be a normal animal, but I'm not aware of her within me, as I am with other life that has lived and died on the hill. She has an existence outside of me. I don't think she has died once yet, if that makes sense."

He stood up and turned his full attention on her. She basked in the heat of his gaze. Its warmth was palpable, and she felt the hairs on her head stirring as if in a slight breeze, or perhaps as if they were growing again at an accelerated rate.

"What I wonder," he said, walking forward to fit his body to hers, "is how long you would live if you stayed on the hill with me. If you left the human world altogether and lived from the spring like me. It might be that, like Flo, you would persist far beyond your normal span. But you burn so brightly, my Sushila. I believe your life would be shortened by the experience. If I am water, you are fire, and I fear that taking you fully into the spring would quench your flame."

He shook his head but didn't speak further. They walked in quiet but companionable silence back to the white cottage, where Sushila put the remaining cat food into the fridge and closed up the house. She paid a brief visit to the bedroom where she patted the wooden box under her bed and made a silent promise. "I haven't forgotten you, Dad," she whispered. "I just need some time to decide what I'm going to do."

They climbed the hill side by side, the little stream chuckling beside them and the skylark singing hosannas in the sunlight. The spring still gushed from its hollow, and the mosses and ferns that fringed the grotto were pale with new growth. Sushila stood facing outwards, pushing her hands into the small of her back and stretching one leg and then the other as she gazed towards the hazy shimmer of the horizon. She sighed comfortably, enjoying the new strength of her body. She turned to her man.

"I didn't bring my walking poles. Didn't even think about it."

"I know." Dougie's voice was tender, but he stared outward into the distance. She slid herself under his arm and hugged him.

"Penny for them."

He stirred, looked down and hugged her back. "Something I need to do. I'm not really looking forward to it."

"Tell me. Is it something I can help with?"

"No, *a ghràidh*. I don't want to talk about it. You help by being here, but I need to deal with this on my own."

He distracted her with kisses, something he'd learned would always work. Sushila castigated herself for being so shallow, but her body responded ardently and they made their way, arm in arm, to Dougie's house.

Almost a full month went by and she hadn't made any decision about leaving. She'd renewed the lease on the car twice and the second time she rented it for a whole month, but it spent most of its time sitting in the yard at the White House, while she was up the hill with Dougie. As the moon waxed again her energies grew. They walked further every day, and so long as he had his hip flask, and she was with him, Dougie seemed to be able to go as far as he wanted from his hill without discomfort. Or, at least, without any discomfort that he was willing to share with her.

He wasn't so much energised as agitated. Whatever was bothering him was growing on his mind, and he wouldn't share it. Often while she was contentedly pottering in her house or his, he would be pacing the floor, unable to settle.

When she drew her attention to his behaviour he settled and made what seemed a conscious effort to still himself. But she could feel the energy seething beneath the surface, like the current of an underground river, and gradually it infected her with the same irritability.

In hindsight, it probably wasn't surprising that it led to their first fight.

It began on the hill, sitting next to the spring. Sushila was using her phone to check connecting flights, trying to sort out a travel package that would see her out to Sri Lanka and back in the shortest time possible. She was trying to decide whether she could get out to sea, scatter Dad's ashes, and be back at the airport in time to fly out on the same day. So far it wasn't working, but she was obsessive about the need to be away for the shortest time possible.

Dougie stood and walked away for a few paces, came back and stood looking down on her. He seemed about to sit down, but changed his mind and walked away again. After several repeats of this behaviour she switched her phone off and stared up at him.

"What is wrong with you?"

He sighed, turned his back and stared out into the distance. She tugged at his hand until she got his attention again. He started to speak, stopped, took a deliberate breath and continued.

"I don't see the point in you only going for a day. You should make a proper trip of it. Really spend some time there and remind yourself of all the reasons you love the place, so that if you decide to stay here you'll be sure you've made the right decision."

"Why are we having this discussion again? I already told you, I know where I want to be. I'll go away and do what needs to be done, but after that I'm coming back to you as soon as I can. I want to spend the rest of my life with you. That is, unless you don't want me?" The tears prickled in her eyes as she considered it. Whatever his reason for raising this again, it felt like rejection.

"Sushila, please don't make this be about emotions."

"Dammit, Dougie, I am emotional. I can't possibly not be emotional about this. I'm so full of conflicting emotions that I feel I'm going to explode, and I'm trying to arrange everything as quickly as I can to bring it all to a close so that I can calm down and move forward without feeling this constant sense of conflict."

"It's the emotion that worries me, *mo ghaoil*. You saw the way the little cat responded to me. There is a glamour, for want of a better word. I feel it working on you when we're together. I want you to go away long enough to get away from my influence. If you are going to come and be here with me, I want to be sure you understand everything you'll be giving up."

"I am not a bloody cat. I'm a fully grown, intelligent, capable human being, and I believe I'm in complete control of my emotions. Yes, I'm attracted to you. Yes, I respond to you. What red-blooded woman wouldn't? But that doesn't mean I'm ruled by animal passions. I want to be with you. Forever. Why is that so hard to understand?"

"I know that. You're probably the smartest woman I've ever known. It's not about that. It's about factors you can't appreciate yet. It's about giving you the space to consider the future without having me so close."

By this time she'd jumped to her feet and was glaring into his face, arms on hips, furious at him for doubting her. She clenched her hands into fists and concentrated on getting her temper under control. When she looked up at him he stepped back a pace and his reaction stung her into speech.

"I'm not going to hurt you." She held out her arms. "Please, let's just kiss and make up. I hate this."

"No. Not this time. If I touch you you'll be happy again. I need you to think."

"Why shouldn't I be happy? Why shouldn't I have a little joy in my life? If you want me and I want you, why does it have to be difficult? I just want it to be what it is."

He held his arms stiffly at his sides and refused to embrace her. His look was sorrowful as he shook his head and turned away. "I'm not going to come to you until you've spent some time thinking about this. You know I'm right. A few months in Sri Lanka won't affect our time together, if that is what's to be. I believe you need to give yourself that long to make your choice."

She turned away, tears blinding her eyes, and stumbled down the hill. "All right," she shouted back over her shoulder. "If you feel that way perhaps we shouldn't see each other for a while."

She looked back at him, daring him to follow her, willing him to give in and come to her. He stood next to the spring, one hand buried in the ferns that overhung the grotto as if drawing strength from it. When she reached the bottom of the hill he was still there, looking out across the empty space between them. Almost she raised a hand to wave to him, but dropped it and turned away, stumbling into the porch where she sat down on the bench and cried until she had no tears left.

That night she lay in her bed, alone for the first time in weeks, unable to sleep. The wind moaned round the newly cleaned chimney and rain pounded on the roof. Lightning flickered through the curtains and she heard the immediate rumble of thunder. It was close.

She climbed out of bed and padded into the kitchen, peering through the window. The rain streamed down the glass and the house was shaken by successive shouts of thunder as the window lit up with the lightning. She was sure the heart of the storm was centred on the hill. Regardless of the superficially controlled mood Dougie had been in when she'd left him earlier, he was having one hell of a paddy now. Sushila's heart ached with absence and she yearned to be with him. Whatever he was feeling, he shouldn't have to feel it alone.

She grabbed jeans and thick socks, hauled her raincoat over her nightdress and pushed her feet into boots. As she opened up the back door the thunder boomed again, shaking the windows. She took two steps into the yard and a bolt of lightning buried itself in the ground in front of her. She felt the light of it pass through her body just as the thunder cracked and shook her to her core. She stumbled back into the kitchen and fell on the kitchen floor. After even such a brief exposure she was soaked to the skin and she examined herself carefully, unable to believe that she hadn't been burned by the lightning. Her heart was racing and beads of sweat stood out on her brow. She couldn't stop shaking.

So much for intervening in the temper tantrum, or whatever the storm represented. She didn't dare risk going up the hill in this. If he didn't realise she was there, and perhaps even if he did, she could easily be struck by the next bolt. She didn't think she would survive that.

The thought brought a realisation home to her. She wasn't ready to die. She wanted beyond all else to join with Dougie and see out eternity with him, but even so, her life was precious to her. No matter that dying on the hill would mean that they could be together, she wasn't ready to let go of the potential her life still held.

With that came calmness and she began to forgive him for trying to drive her away. He stood to gain nothing by persuading her to leave. He was only thinking about her needs. She stripped off the wet clothes and climbed back into her bed, hearing the thunder rumble above her head. The storm seemed to be passing over and the rain settled to a steady downpour. Perhaps the tantrum was over?

Much later in the night, as the sky paled towards dawn and the blackbird in the garden sounded his opening note in the dawn chorus, the door opened and a cool body slid in beside her. She turned to him and opened herself and they came together as sweetly and quietly as the falling rain. Afterwards, he cradled her in his arms and she listened to the calm, steady rhythm of his heart.

"I'm sorry. I never meant to hurt you."

Either of them could have spoken it.

1955

The man walked up the main street, noting changes. There were a lot more vehicles around, for a start. He jumped as a lorry hooted at him, its driver apparently incensed that this elderly pedestrian was wandering up the middle of the road. Donald shifted the heavy canvas kit bag to his other shoulder and moved onto the pavement. He hardly noticed its weight. He'd been accustomed to shifting his worldly goods from ship to ship his whole adult life.

He admired the figures of two young women as he stepped briefly off the kerb to let them past. Their midlength skirts showed their calves and two fine pairs of button boots. He nodded to them and raised his cap as they went by. He didn't recognise their features, but the old gent reclining outside the village hall, with an unlit pipe clamped between his teeth, looked like somebody's father. Fraser maybe, or MacInnes? He wasn't ready yet to seek out people he'd once known. There was something he needed to do first.

The walk up to the cemetery was long and steep, and Donald felt his legs and back aching long before he reached its low stone wall. Around the border of the churchyard bright daffodils nodded, and the grass between the gravestones was a rich green. Donald dropped his kit bag at the gate and went in. He was pretty sure he'd find him here.

It wasn't as easy as that, though.

Almost an hour later he'd walked the cemetery through and looked at every grave marker. There was no sign of his brother. The telegram had been brief, but clear:

Dougal dead. Come home.

He'd assumed it had come from Maire Fannon. Who else would have any idea what ship he might be on, or in which port his mail might find him? Now, he wasn't so sure. He'd found Maire's grave all right.

Maire MacLean, beloved wife of Dougal MacLean. 1897-1916

So the message couldn't have come from her. It didn't look as though they'd had much time together. But where was his brother, if not here?

He jumped at a slight noise beside him, and looked down to see a small hand in a grey glove laid on his wrist. It belonged to the elderly woman he'd seen arriving a few minutes ago, with flowers in hand. He'd stayed his distance from her, not wanting to intrude on someone else's grief.

"Hello, Donald."

He looked at her more closely. Small and slim, she was not as old as he'd first thought. Around his own age, in fact. At this realisation, the features of her face triggered a memory and he reflexively straightened.

"Eilidh MacDonald. I beg your pardon, I did not recognise you."

His retreat into formality masked a moment of sheer terror. He well remembered the last time he'd seen his one-time sweetheart, and the parting words he'd shared with his brother. Faced with the possibility that he'd got his girlfriend pregnant he'd done the only thing he could bear to do: he'd run away.

Eilidh's eyes were still on him, and he forced himself to meet her gaze. She smiled and, turning, linked her arm in his. "Dougie's not here," she said. "Come on, I'll take you home. There's a lot to explain, and I need a cup of tea."

Bewildered, Donald picked up his kit bag as they left the graveyard and escorted her where she wanted to go.

In the little house on the hill, high above the rooftops

and clock tower of the town, Donald sat uncomfortably in a flowered armchair while Eilidh busied herself making the tea. He looked round the room, cosy with the possessions of a woman who lived alone. There were no wedding photographs, apart from one very old sepia daguerreotype of her parents in their best clothes. They stared disapprovingly at the boy who'd taken advantage of their daughter, not at all welcoming the prodigal's return.

In pride of place on the mantelpiece sat the photograph of a young man, no more than twenty years old or so, bright-eyed and fresh-faced in a thick fisherman's jersey and cotton cap. He grinned out of the picture, and Donald tried not to resent that his replacement had turned out to be such a good looking chap. Eilidh nodded at the picture as she set out the teacups.

"That's my son," she said. "Archie, after my father."

Donald looked again. Now he could see a resemblance between the laughing man and the dour face in the old portrait. They had the same nose, long and straight, but the boy's smile came straight from Eilidh herself.

She sat down beside him and laid her hand on his arm again. "I sent the telegram," she said. "I assume that's why you came home."

He looked at her, and covered his confusion with a joke. "It hasn't been my home for a long time."

She nodded, taking the comment seriously. "Dougie didn't have anyone else. After your grandmother died, and then Maire and the babe, he stayed on the hill by himself. I tried to persuade him to move to town, but he wasn't for shifting. Too many memories up there. I think he liked to lose himself in them.

"About two years ago he stopped coming down, even for his bit of shopping. I went up to the house a few times, to see if he was ill, but he wasn't there. I thought he must have finally found the same wanderlust that bit you, though I was surprised he'd go away without telling me. We were friends, you see. I'd done for him after Maire died, to help him get back on his feet, and he was very supportive when Archie…"

Her voice trailed off, and he looked down to see a tear fall from her bent head onto his trousers. She straightened her shoulders and went on.

"All my boy ever wanted was to go out on the fishing. He loved the sea. He started with crabbing off the pier and collecting limpets to sell for bait, but as soon as he was old enough he persuaded one of the trawlermen to take him on. The sea was his life. In the end it took his life." She pulled a handkerchief out of her sleeve and dabbed at her eyes. "It was his grave I was visiting when I saw you."

Donald looked into Eilidh's eyes and felt a great swell of compassion. He hadn't quite put it all together yet, but he knew a grieving woman when he saw one. He held out his arms and she bowed her head and slumped into them, allowing herself to cry. The slight weight of her, and the warmth of her body in his arms, stirred an old, old memory and he lowered his head and brushed a kiss over her hair.

Eilidh sat up again, and took a sip of her tea. She tidied herself, putting her grief aside, and went back to her story. "It was only last autumn that Dougie was found. He'd died up there on the top of the mountain, and his poor body had lain out with the ravens for heaven knows how long. He was all gone to bones, but they knew him by his clothes. He's buried on the hill, in the old village graveyard. I thought he would like that."

Donald nodded, remembering the brother who stayed. "He never wanted to leave the hill," he said.

Eilidh sat back in her own chair and nibbled a piece of shortbread.

He glanced at her, remembering her fine, straight figure and the glossy highlights in her hair, now a faded grey. She was still a looker, after all these years. He thought he'd figured it all out, but felt a compulsion to make sure.

"So, how did Maire feel about the two of you?"

"How do you mean?"

"Well, he married her, but he was still friends with you. I presume…" He nodded at the picture of Archie, as good-looking as you might expect from a liaison between his handsome brother and the beautiful and desirable Eilidh MacDonald.

Eilidh huffed, and leaned forward as she put down her teacup. He sat back in his seat as her body moved towards his and she looked him straight in the eye.

"Donald MacLean, don't be an idiot. There was only ever one man for me."

15
☽ MOUNTAIN ☾

June saw them trying out their riskiest trick yet. They rose at dawn and climbed into the car, Sushila kissing Dougie on the nose before closing her door and losing him. She was growing accustomed to the empty feeling in the pit of her stomach that she got whenever it happened. So far he'd always been there whenever they arrived at their destination, and she willed herself to remain confident that the same would happen again.

The drive round to the foot of the big mountain took a little under an hour, giving her plenty of time to think through the planned programme for the day. Halfway there she realised she'd forgotten to pack a raincoat and nearly turned back, but the few clouds in the sky were thin and high, and it looked as if it was going to be another hot, dry day. She worried about how they would handle the mountain, but the feeling in her stomach was as much excitement as fear. It was good to be trying something new.

She'd been tucked up in the curve of Dougie's body two nights before, drowsy and satiated after sex but somehow not quite sleepy enough to drop off, when he'd made the suggestion.

"Why don't we climb the Ben?"

She squirmed round to look him in the face. "That's over three thousand feet. I've never done anything like that before. Don't you have to be some kind of die-hard mountaineer?"

"Not at all. It's just a big hill. You start at the bottom and keep walking till you get to the top. I've always wanted to climb it. In the winter I sit on my hill and look at it, all stark and snow-covered, and I wonder what it's like. Anyway, it would be a good test of how much your leg has improved."

"Too right it would. If I can climb the Ben I can probably cope with anything life sends me. But can you go that far? It would mean being away from the spring for a whole day. What if you can't cope with that?"

"I'll be the first to let you know if I'm in trouble. As long as we take plenty of spring water with us I should be all right, and it would give me the chance to see if there's any life on the mountain. I've always thought that if there were any others like me I couldn't do better than to start with the tallest mountain on the island. I'd like to feel its energies."

So it was decided. Now that the time had come Sushila wasn't at all convinced she was going to make it all the way to the top. She tried not to worry that the dry, clear weather might affect Dougie. He was big enough to look after himself, and after all they'd just spent weeks testing his limits without finding any outer edge to them: a powerful contrast to his original expectations. Had his limits changed over the decades, or was it that things were different when they were together? They'd planned for all possible contingencies; he should be all right today.

She pulled up on the grass verge next to the loch. That early in the morning there was no-one on the mountain yet, although there was a camper van parked a few hundred yards away. She looked around to check that no-one was in sight and opened her door. To her relief Dougie's grin greeted her.

"Like the bloody Cheshire Cat," she grumbled. He smirked and unfolded himself from the passenger seat, stretching his long arms up into the sky before checking his pack to make sure none of the water bottles leaked. He had a whole bag full of plastic sports-cap bottles retrieved from the MacDougalls' recycling bin. Sushila too was carrying water from the spring, along with sandwiches and apples and a small first aid kit. She was banking on the mountain being so well-climbed that they wouldn't need a map, but she'd brought a little booklet that described the climb, just in case.

Their journey began with a gentle walk up a metalled track, before passing through a gate and onto the hill. The route more-or-less followed a stream that came off the mountain, still rushing with water despite the dryness of the day: a busy, noisy water broken at regular intervals by waterfalls and rapids. When the track dropped to the stream edge Dougie bent and took a mouthful of the water. He rolled it round inside his mouth like an expert wine taster, but swallowed rather than spat. Sushila looked at him and quirked an eyebrow. He shrugged and kept walking.

They tramped on, slowly gaining height, following the stream along the way. After about forty minutes Sushila sank down on a boulder and pulled out a bottle. She limited herself to a couple of mouthfuls, having learned from her surfing days that wetting the mouth is often all that's needed. Dougie, on the other hand, waded into a green pool at the base of a waterfall and ducked his head under the water. He came out looking like a wet dog, shaking the water from his hair in an energetic cascade that reached all the way to where she was sitting. "Oi! Watch out," she told him.

He shook himself dry and bent over her. "I can dry you if you want," he said, "but you might find further up the mountain that being damp keeps you cool."

"That's all right. No need to show off." She gazed at him affectionately; admiring the way the sun shone through his curls and lit up his face. "How is the water? Are you feeling anything?"

"It's an old, old mountain, I get that right enough, but I can't tell if there's any presence here. I may need to get right up onto the slopes before I can be sure."

She stood and put her hands on her hips, looking upwards in the direction of their destination. As they climbed, the foothills swallowed up the peak, until all she could see ahead of her was a stretch of hillside topped by a cairn of small stones. There was no way to ascertain how far they had yet to go. She shrugged her pack back onto her shoulders and started off again.

Dougie was right. Climbing in the sun was hot, and the water he'd sprayed on her soon evaporated. The small of her back was sweaty and the back of her neck felt overheated, and as she walked she pulled a bottle of sun cream out of her pocket and anointed her neck and the tops of her ears. She wondered whether a ghost could get sunburn.

It was very difficult to understand how anything in the environment affected him. Why did he disappear when the car's doors were closed, and not when he sat down and lifted his feet off the ground? It wasn't logical. He could soak himself to the skin one moment, and shake off the water and be completely dry the next, the implication being that he had almost complete control over what physical forces affected him and what didn't. He was fully palpable to her, while at the same time apparently invisible to anyone else. And yet they could touch, and interact, as easily as two completely human people. There was nothing imaginary or other-worldly about that.

"An enigma wrapped in a bacon roll," she muttered to herself, baring her teeth in a half-grin as he caught the sound of the words and glanced over at her.

The constant uphill slope began to tell on her as they continued to press forward. At first she ignored the twinges in her leg, telling herself they were imaginary, but as the morning wore on she had to admit that she was feeling it. The left leg was much better than it had been, but it wasn't as robust as the right. When she finally admitted to Dougie that she was in trouble he gave up trotting in and out of the stream and came to her side, obviously concerned. He made her sit down and stretch her legs, took them in his hands and massaged them from calf to thigh. After that he poured a little spring water into his hands and rubbed that into her skin. When he'd finished she felt a lot better, and instead of pain her legs were glowing with a heat that seemed to come from within.

They reached a point where the track turned away from the stream and Sushila expected that when they reached the next cairn they would have crossed the ridge they were climbing, and a vista of the mountain would open out before them. But all she found when she reached that point was another stretch of boulder-strewn hillside and another pile of rocks on the horizon, beckoning her upwards. Her breath was coming quickly now and she could feel her heartbeat thudding in her temples. She paused to look over at Dougie. He looked no different now that they'd left the stream, and it didn't seem he'd taken any energy from it. If he had, he certainly wasn't talking about it.

She set her sights on the next cairn and plodded on, and after that to the next and the next. At last they found themselves zigzagging up a broad slope of scree that crumbled away under their feet and made walking even more difficult. Sushila found she needed to stop more frequently and Dougie spent more time working on her legs and keeping her going. Despite the problems she was amazed at how far they'd come. They paused long enough to eat an apple and admire the view.

Far below her the car looked like a black dot at the edge of the loch. She could see vast currents swirling in the water, and pale turquoise patches where the sea bottom was sand instead of rock. The sun stood out in the vault of heaven without a cloud left to give them shelter, and the temperature had risen sharply. Sushila panted in the heat. She glanced over at Dougie, catching him unawares. His head was hanging and he had one hand pressed to his side.

"Hey. You're supposed to tell me if you get into trouble."

"I'm all right." He panted and bent forward, resting his hands on his knees. Sushila opened his pack and pulled out a bottle of spring water, twisting off the top and pouring the contents over his head. He gasped as the water hit him, but immediately looked better. "Thank you. I hadn't thought of that."

"It's what we brought it for, I thought."

"I'd forgotten I had it. Getting stupid in my old age. Or maybe it's the altitude." He grinned at her, but she still didn't like the look of him.

"We can turn back. Just say. There's no point in taking risks."

"No. I want to do it. We've come all this way. It can't be much further now."

He wedged himself onto the rock beside her and shared his sweaty warmth with her, grinning when she shoved him away. Now they'd stopped moving the intense quiet of the landscape seeped into her consciousness, and she became aware that apart from the distant murmur of the stream and a faint breath of wind across her ears there was virtually no sound. She shook her head, as if to clear it. In her ears a faint drumming sound intruded. At first she thought it was the sound of her own heartbeat, but the sound swelled and died in a peculiar way. It sounded as if it was coming from outside her.

She looked around and shook her head again, wondering if it was an insect close to her ear. For a moment all was still, then the sound came again: its source was above her. Tipping her head back, Sushila gazed into the sky. The sound came again, and this time she saw the small shape swooping out of the sky and pulling up into level flight as the drumming ceased. She watched it rise, wings beating hard, and then it dropped and the rhythmic sound repeated.

Dougie put back his head too, and they sat in silence and watched the strange little bird. Sushila searched her memory of walks with her father, but couldn't remember anything like this. She looked at Dougie and he smiled back.

"It's a snipe," he said. "I haven't heard one for years. The drum sound comes from the air moving through the bird's feathers; males make the sound to mark their territory, or possibly to impress the girls."

"Impressing the girls being something that every male worth his salt needs to be able to do." She cocked her head to one side as she looked at him, her mouth quirked. He bent and kissed its irresistible softness.

"Is there anything more important than that?" He stood and held out his hand to pull her to her feet.

The track led on before them, marked out at regular intervals by more cairns. Each time they passed one, Sushila added a stone to the pile created by previous walkers. The sun climbed higher in the sky and it grew hotter and hotter. So far they were the only climbers on the Ben, and at times it seemed they were toiling up an endless slope that steadily grew steeper as the temperature increased. They took two further stops, and each time Dougie drank and poured the spring water over his head.

Logic told Sushila that they were making progress, but each landmark achieved revealed only another stretch of slope with a cairn or pile of boulders ahead. Her leg had improved after Dougie's first treatment, but still he made sure to repeat it each time they paused to rest.

On they climbed, step by step up the flank of the mountain, leaning hands on knees to stabilise them as they alternated large steps up piled boulders with shuffling movements across scree slopes. Slowly but surely they gained altitude, but Sushila was becoming steadily more worried about Dougie. He'd poured the last bottle of spring water over himself a few paces back and he was still struggling. The air was dry and superheated, and there was no prospect of shelter further on. Again Sushila suggested going back, but he shook his head stubbornly and she turned and walked on to the next cairn.

This time the track entered what must surely be the final push, up a steep ridge between slopes of scree. There was still quite a climb to come, and this section was even steeper than those which had come before. Sushila downed a mouthful of water as Dougie made his way to her side. After one look at his face she held out the bottle and he swallowed its contents convulsively. She took back the empty bottle and looked worriedly at him. He shook his head.

"*Mo chridhe*," he said, his face distorted by discomfort, and reached towards her. "I'm sorry." And in a heartbeat he was gone.

Sushila gasped and put her hand to her mouth. There'd been no warning. A little, hot breath of air touched her face and whispered away down the hill. She sat down as her legs gave way beneath her.

"Oh, Dougie."

She sat for about ten minutes, waiting to see if there would be any change. It took her that long to stop shaking. She thought about all the possibilities they had planned for. She'd never imagined it could happen without any warning at all. Or had Dougie had that warning? Was he so focused on getting her to the top of the hill that he'd been prepared to overlook the signs? Or had it been as surprising to him as it was to her? And, most importantly of all, where was he?

Sushila sat and chewed over her surmises and best guesses. She wanted to rush down the slope and back home as fast as she possibly could. She needed to know he was okay. But as she sat and thought she rejected the worst case scenario. Dougie was gone and there was nothing she could do about that.

Don't think about that. It's crippling. Assume he can get home. He will be there when you arrive. You are so close to the summit. He would want you to finish the job. All right then.

She pulled herself to her feet and set off up the ridge. It was so steep that sometimes she slid back almost as far as she'd climbed. As she went she heard voices and realised that another team of climbers was coming up fast behind her. Thank goodness they hadn't come across her and Dougie a few minutes earlier. It would have been unbearable if Dougie had disappeared in front of other people (who couldn't see him anyway) leaving her to pretend nothing had happened when all the time her heart was breaking.

Her left leg was seriously aching, and she began to realise how much Dougie had been supporting her throughout the climb. That must have contributed to his loss of energy, as much as the effort of surviving in such a dry environment. Rather than making her feel guilty, the thought spurred her on. She was damned if his sacrifice was going to be for nothing. She owed it to him to complete the climb.

The last few steps up the ridge were harder than any before, but when she raised her head she found herself stumbling onto a broad, flat summit surmounted by a huge cairn. She trudged forward and added a stone of her own to the cairn just as the other climbers summited beside her. She watched them slapping each other on the back and sharing out chocolate before turning her back on them and the Ben and starting the long trudge down again. She couldn't bring herself to share their delight.

1973

The air was crisp and cool on his face. Blowing from the sea across the fields below, when it reached him he could taste hay, brine, horse manure, a hint of flowers. It thrummed gently in his ears, but the chuckle of the stream was closer, and louder. His hands clenched and opened, clutching at the turf on which he lay. The sudden reek of grass and earth filled his nostrils. He sneezed and sat up.

A wave of disappointment washed across his mind. He was not dead. Wearily, he set himself to endure another endless day of breathing and living. He dragged himself painfully to his feet. No. Wait.

This was different. He rose without difficulty, stood breathing without pain. His eyes opened and he saw, clear and sharp before him, the stream and hillside of his home. Above him, cloud coated the hilltops. A few shreds of mist hung around him, and he sensed the cloud was thickening. He paused and consulted his internal clock.

It was late on an autumn afternoon. The smells on the wind, the feel of the day, the sun already sinking into cloud behind him—all these things agreed with his inner sense of time. If anything, he felt more confident than ever. Something told him that this day bore more significance than most. If his internal sense could be trusted, it was Samhainn, the autumn equinox: the eve when the dead walk.

Well, of course that made sense. He'd laid himself down on the hillside late on Samhainn evening, bats flitting from their caves, land falling quiet into dusk, glad to die, and be at peace.

Obviously he hadn't died. That didn't make sense, either,

for now it was earlier in the day. Could his time sense be wrong? He rummaged inside himself, feeling blindly for the place in his mind where time lay. No, he wasn't wrong. It was Samhainn again. He just knew.

Frustrated, Dougie clenched his fists and kicked a rock. Pain shocked through him, and he looked down to see blood on his bare toes. Toes he hadn't seen without wincing for decades. Toes that were pink, and well-shaped and, frankly, young. He grasped at his body, becoming aware that he was naked. Where his hands expected wrinkled skin, slack muscle and the stooping stance he'd adopted in his later years, he found instead strength, suppleness—life. If his was death, he liked it. Whooping, he gave way to a rush of euphoria and ran headlong down the hill towards his house.

Reaching it, he sobered immediately. There was no house. Two or three courses of stone stood proud from the rock, with the dark cave behind. Many more large stones lay scattered in the long grass, and the porch stone rested, as it always had, outside the front door—or where the door should have been. This was not the work of a night. This kind of decay took years.

He squatted on the porch stone, absently stroking his hand across its smoothness, while he thought. This didn't feel like death. His foot hurt where he'd stubbed it, his skin was cooling as the evening came on, he had nothing with which to clothe his nakedness: he was hungry. If this was some kind of special hell thought up for Dougal MacLean it was a very strange one, joy and terror mixed in with a kind of desperate loneliness. Not so different from his life, in fact.

The wind shifted direction and blew cold droplets across his body. He shivered, and sneezed. Darkness was falling fast, the blanket of cloud sinking over the hill, laden with moisture. Dougie shifted himself into the shelter of the cave, stooping under the hill, and tucked himself into a corner, as far from the entrance as he could get. Outside, the wind began to moan. Curled around himself, shuddering with the cold, he set himself to survive the night.

Later, his eyes opened to the shifting shadows and leaping half-light of a fire. His body opened itself gratefully to the warmth until he noticed the others. Shrinking back, he tried to cover his bareness, hunching a shoulder to the presences while his body continued to yearn for the heat radiating from the centre of the cave. Outside, the wind continued to howl, but a thick drape of woollen cloth hung from the entrance and broke the draughts.

"Cover yourself, child." The woman's voice was harsh, disapproving.

"I'm sorry," he said. "I have no clothing."

She flicked one impatient finger, and Dougie gratefully drew a thick, woollen blanket around his shoulders. She grunted. "I had thought trousers," she said, amused. "Interesting, what parts you most wish to protect."

The other figure leaned forward and stirred the embers with a stick, reaching behind to grasp a log and add it to the blaze. His arm in the firelight was blue with tattoos. Dougie felt a sharp sense of recognition. The other nodded his head, turning his face towards the light. His profile was thin, imperious—smiling. "Yes, you know me, child."

The woman stood and moved around the fire towards him. She held a wooden bowl, crudely carved. She gave it to him and he drank, wondering what poison it contained. He didn't care. The day could become no stranger than it already was.

The bowl contained water. It slipped down his throat, cool and heady, and he felt the hairs on his head stand up. It filled him, until he was neither hungry nor thirsty. He gave the bowl back to the woman and smiled his thanks. She nodded to him, seeming suddenly less intimidating, and sat down again, smoothing her skirts. He noticed her bare feet peeping out, but she seemed unaffected by the cold, as did the other figure which, now that he came to look at it, appeared not to be wearing any clothing either. He, unlike

Dougie, seemed unashamed to be seen so.

He took a closer look at the woman. She was much younger than he'd taken her for, no more than a girl, perhaps in her late teens. She wore a long woollen skirt and a leather jerkin, and her arms were bare. Barely visible under the shoulder of the jerkin, a blue tattoo flowed down her upper arm. He got the feeling that it continued, unseen, beneath her clothes. The firelight flickered and he looked into her eyes. For a moment he felt himself falling into dark water, the surface closing over his head. He felt himself drowning, and grasped vainly for comprehension as she cocked her head and spoke to the old man, in a language he did not understand. Her voice was familiar, but it was by her eyes he knew her.

"Grandmother," he said.

"Well, so, the child has some small wisdom." Her voice was sour. It gave him the familiar sense of having disappointed her.

The blue man shifted, and his movement drew Dougie's gaze. As soon as his grandmother's eyes released him he felt himself begin to breathe again. Soon, the dark spots before his eyes faded and he felt calmer.

"Do not torment the boy, *a nighean*. He does not yet understand."

"And well do I know that. A lifetime spent teaching that boy. The best part of a century in the waiting for him, and when he comes, all he knows to do is to play at human love."

The old man snorted in laughter and she rounded on him. "It was not the same for me. I needed the man to get the child. That is the way of it." She glared at him, like a little wildcat cornered.

"It was the same," he said. He held her eye, calm and unmoved, until she subsided, flicking her skirts around herself as she settled back into her corner.

Dougie met the man's gaze in turn, and sank into the misted depths of an ancient well, deep as compassion.

Fragments of a thousand lifetimes played across his memory, and the sweep and pattern of his own life lay spread out before him. He blinked, emerging from his trance, and re-examined the events of the day. Now he understood. As he stirred, he realised that he wore clothing: breeks, a soft shirt, and one of the grey sweaters his wife had made for him. His feet were warm in thick, woollen socks. He remembered Maire knitting them, swearing as she struggled to turn the heel.

"I had forgotten," he said, wondering.

"Indeed." His grandmother's voice was still abrasive.

Dougie remembered her too: taking him into her house when his mother died; teaching him her songs; showing him the strange ways of the water, the earth and the light; setting the tattoo into his back, and singing him, pinprick by pinprick, all the lineage of his people.

He tried to explain. "I did it for Maire. She would never have understood. She needed me to be a man like other men. I loved her."

His grandmother's expression softened. "They are easy to love," she said.

16
☽ ABSENCE AND LOSS ☾

The journey back down took her two hours. Every step produced an incremental increase in pain, and by the time she reached the lower slopes the process seemed interminable. Partway down the steep scree slope she leaned too heavily on one of her walking poles and it broke. Whatever internal mechanism held the pole at full length gave way and the pole slid into itself, failing to provide any support at all.

Sushila propped herself on a rock and tried to mend it. She pulled the pole back out to the length she wanted and tightened the grip. It seemed to be fine, but the moment she leaned any weight on it the grip gave way and it slithered back into itself. The mechanism seemed simple, and yet her thoughts were so sluggish that she couldn't figure out what was going wrong. She spent the rest of the slow scramble down relying on one pole, while using the other to fend off boulders whenever they came within its shortened reach. In some places the drop from one step to the next was so steep that her battered knees could no longer cope with it, and she had to sit down and shuffle herself over the drop.

The lower slopes of the mountain were boggy, and her footing uncertain. She plodded onwards, squishing through the damp patches, but slipping only once. Her feet slid out from under her, and she found herself lying on her back in a muddy hollow, laughing hysterically, before pulling herself together and going on.

The final moments of her ordeal came when she reached the track at the bottom of the hill. Even here, where the slope was minimal, she was able only to take shuffling steps, hips and knees stiff with pain, but at last she reached the road and her waiting vehicle. She lowered herself gingerly into the driver's seat, put the key in the ignition and wound down all the windows. The inside of the car was like an oven, and the seat leather was blistering, but she hardly noticed. Putting her head down on the steering wheel, she let a few tears sting her eyes. She had tried not to let herself hope that Dougie would be there. But hope there had been, nonetheless, and its disappointment was bitter.

She paused long enough to change out of her walking boots and to stash her pack and poles in the boot. A half-empty and nastily warm bottle of water served to rehydrate her and she set off, sternly determined to keep her attention on the road and not think about what awaited her back home. Dougie's face, briefly contorted with discomfort in the moment before he evaporated before her eyes, swam across her inner vision, but she blinked it away and pulled out onto the road.

Fifty long minutes later she swung the little car across the cattle grid and into the dusty yard. Sushila hauled herself wearily out of her seat and set off up the hill. The short rest had done nothing to heal the overuse of her muscles, other than to stiffen her up slightly, and her left leg ached with a pain driven deep into the bone. She ignored it. The pain held at bay by the lines incised on her forehead, and by her determination not to accept what she feared, was so great that mere body aches were unimportant. She pushed herself up the climb, scrambling on hands and feet, desperate to reach the spring.

There was no-one there.

Sushila sat beside the spring, unshed tears burning behind her eyes, for the rest of the afternoon. Slowly the sun left the hill and the temperature began to drop. The little spring chuckled merrily as it sprang over the lip of its pool and poured itself down the hill. Clouds on the eastern horizon glowed pink as the sun slipped away in the west. A cool breeze arose and whispered through the grass, but its voice was wordless and had nothing to say to her. At last she stirred and stood, making her way wearily down the steep slope to her empty, silent house.

She dragged a blanket back up the hill and spent the night beside the spring. The ground was dry and there was little moisture in the atmosphere, but the hollow of the spring was cool and airy. Somewhere in the long watches of the night, tears came, burned through her in an eruption of grief, and dried again on her cheeks when at last the reservoir of emotion ran dry. She sat on, staring into the darkness, the astonishing beauty of starlight cutting her like blades. At last, worn out by fear and hope, she lay down on the cool turf and slept.

She woke to find her face and hair wet with dew. As she came back to consciousness she realised that her head was pillowed on a warm surface. Her body was wrapped in a slightly damp blanket and she was being held, closely and firmly, by a pair of strong and familiar arms. She rolled over on her stomach, pulling herself free of the embrace, and met the warmth of Dougie's gaze. He was lying flat on his back on the hard ground with his feet pointing at the sky, as relaxed and comfortable as if he'd been on his bed at home.

She stared at him, hardly daring to breath, and then reached out to touch his shoulder. Finding it as warm and tangible as any man's she lost her temper and punched his arm.

"How could you do that? How could you frighten me that way? I hate you, I hate you."

He lay unmoving, allowing her to hit him. For all that he could probably let the blows pass straight through him if he wished, it was clear from his occasional winces that she was hurting him. With that the anger dissipated as quickly as it had arisen, and Sushila threw herself on his body. His arms encircled her again and held her tight as she tried to press her body as close to his as it was humanly possible to get. A storm of tears shook her and he stroked her hair gently until it passed.

"It's all right, *mo chridhe*. I'm still here. No harm done."

Eventually the words penetrated her distress and she calmed herself. She sat up again and scrubbed her face with her hands, running her fingers through her hair to detangle it. With every passing moment she was becoming more secure in his presence, no longer fearing that he was a figment of her dreaming mind. She felt damp and chilled after a night on the hill, and the tangle of her hair was getting in her eyes. She was definitely awake. He was definitely here.

With that the anger surfaced again, although this time it was cooler and more controlled. "How can I know this isn't going to happen again? Dougie, I was really frightened. I thought you might have lost yourself on the mountain, that you might never come home. We can't afford to try anything like that again. I don't think I can cope with the fear of losing you."

He lay still, looking up at her, his face unperturbed, apparently unaffected by her emotional outburst. Quietly, he muttered, "If you love something, set it free."

"What?"

He laughed. "1970s cod philosophy," he said.

She stared at him for a moment. Then the import of what he'd said filtered through to her and she thumped the ground with her fist, exasperated.

"All right, I suppose I take your point. You don't want your actions to be controlled by me. Fair enough. But you've done more travelling in the last few weeks than in all the decades you've lived on this hill. Haven't you seen enough now?"

"No." His voice was firm. "If you want to keep me, you have to let me go. Each of us has restrictions on our choices, born of our pasts as well as our natures. Each of us has to agree to allow the other to be free to make decisions. Even if some of them hurt. Without that we simply don't have a partnership."

Slowly, she nodded. "Okay. I don't like it, but I agree." She leaned forward and ran her hands lightly across his face, then bent and touched her mouth to his. The kiss was slow and soft and she felt the slow burn of desire reaching its tendrils outward from her groin.

"But can we at least agree that you won't do anything risky today? I don't think I could bear it."

"Agreed."

He ran his fingers up the back of her neck and into her hair. She closed her eyes as his touch released the last of the tension from the top of her spine. He nuzzled her ear, then lay back and put his hands behind his head. His eyes gleamed. "So, did you get to the top?"

"Of course." She sat up and poked him in the breastbone to add emphasis. "I had to do the job on my own while you went home for a nice rest."

His hands on her wrists were strong and hard as he pushed her weight off him and rolled over on top of her. She gasped as his lips came down on hers and she wrapped her legs around his thighs. A rock made its presence felt in the small of her back and she wriggled to escape the sharp pain, but as soon as she thought about it she felt the solid projection melt away and the turf beneath her became as soft and yielding as a mattress. She could feel his arousal in the pit of her stomach, as well as its physical manifestation pressing against her abdomen.

Today it was her turn to demonstrate self-control. After a few moments of passionate kissing, while he showed his desire to get as close to her as two sets of clothing would allow, she wriggled out from underneath and jumped to her feet. She put her hand out to his and hauled him upwards, pulling him in the direction of his house. If they were going to have a proper reunion in broad daylight, it was going to be done behind closed doors.

As they made their way across the hilltop, something occurred to her. "Hold on, Mr MacLean. You claim you died in 1953. How do you know anything about the 1970s?

Dougie let go of her hand and took her by the waist to swing her over the stream. He continued to hold on to her while they made their way down the slope towards his porch, so she tucked her own arm into his elbow and leaned into him.

"Oh, that's easy. Though sad, I suppose."

She stopped walking and looked up into his face. She already had an inkling of what he was going to say.

"A child died here about twenty years ago. He was a summer visitor, staying in one of the cottages round the far slope of the hill. His childhood had been a good one, with caring parents and an older sister who loved him to bits. She was the one who read to him, and so his head was full of all her favourite stories. And a child who has been ill all his life has a great sympathy for tales of alternative universes, especially ones in which death is the enemy.

"He comforted himself with tales of his heroes, from Orpheus and Theseus to rock singers like Marc Bolan and Jim Morrison. It wasn't lost on him that meeting death in a heroic fashion was not the same thing as defeating it."

"How do you feel about that?" Sushila found herself struggling with an aspect of Dougie's life that she hadn't examined before. "Given that you're effectively immortal."

"I'm not. It's not like that. There was a beginning to this life I've inherited, long ago in human times but the blink of an eye in the lifespan of the earth. And it will end. Perhaps not until the hills are ground into dust and disappear beneath the sea, but the end will come. One day."

Sushila swallowed a lump in her throat and nodded, but didn't speak as he went on, "They came here on holiday. It was supposed to be a special vacation for all of them, but most especially for the boy, because they knew that he faced more treatment and it was going to be very hard. He didn't want it. It hurt so much the last time, and he didn't think he could stand any more. He managed to hide from his parents how much pain he was in. Even his sister had only an inkling of the truth.

"He understood what was wrong with him. Leukaemia. He knew it was killing him, and that all their treatments had failed to conquer the disease. The only real hope was a bone marrow transplant, but that required a suitable donor and none of his family were compatible. And, anyway, in those days the transplant itself was a very dangerous and painful procedure, with no certain promise of success. He lay in his bed that last night, knowing that his holiday was nearly over and he would have to summon great strength to endure what was ahead. In the end he summoned that strength of will and purpose and turned it to another use: he chose to die.

"I didn't know anything about him until I felt him come into me. Of all those who have died on the hill over the centuries, before me and after, he is one of the strongest and the most complete. I can still feel the strength of purpose and the vast creative imagination that he brought into the world; it's part of me, and I gained immeasurably by it. It's through him that I know what little I do of twentieth century literature, and much else about the modern world besides."

She shivered. "So, is that how it works? Nothing after death except for people who die on this hill, and they are subsumed into the almost immortal presence that is Dougal MacLean?"

"No. It's not like that at all." Dougie shook his head in distress. "It's only the memories that I have. I felt the boy go. He gave me everything but his essential self, and that went free, leaving the pain clean behind. I honour him for it."

Sushila was sombre. There was something touching and brave about the story of this boy. "What was his name?"

"Aidan."

"What happened to his family, afterwards?"

"I don't know. Apart from you, my darling, I feel almost nothing from the living. They don't become real to me until they die."

She shivered. For a moment she almost comprehended the vast loneliness inherent in that comment, but they had reached the house and he swept her inside and pushed the door closed behind him, bending his head immediately to take her lips and make her his again. Sushila fended him off. She wasn't finished.

"So when I asked you if you'd ever worked on the ferry, and you said 'a long time ago', who was that really?"

"Oh, that was my brother. He was never going to stay at home with Gran. First chance he got he went off to work on the ferry. That was on the wee MacBrayne ferry that used to run the round trip between the mainland and three of the islands. These days there's a big ferry coming in further south. That's the one you caught, I presume?"

She nodded and he went on, "My brother lasted a few months on the local ferry, with stints in between on fishing boats and back here on the hill. He took me hunting and taught me his moonshine brewing skills, but it wasn't long before he got a proper job in the merchant navy, and left home for good. When he retired from the sea he came home to the hill and boarded with a woman round on the eastern flank of the hill, overlooking the town. That was after I died, though. The last time I saw him alive was when we were both still very young.

"When I came back to myself at the side of the spring and discovered I'd been given a new life, my brother was already part of me. It was then I discovered that the woman he'd been boarding with had been his lover. I was sorry he was gone, but I was glad to know he'd lived a happy life, and that he was not afraid to die."

He looked at her with concern in his eyes, but relaxed as he confirmed that she wasn't shocked. Sushila's gaze was as warm and trusting as ever. She reached up and pulled his face down to hers and he lifted her and carried her through to the pile of sheepskins and blankets that made up his bed. There he did his best to make her forget the fear and distress of the day before.

***

When at last she lay sated and drowsy, head pillowed on his chest as he stroked her slowly into sleep, he allowed himself a brief moment of guilt. He didn't think she'd been aware of his subtle drawing of power from her during their lovemaking. Tomorrow she might guess when she felt the surge of energy that followed their joining. His loss of substance up the Ben, and the subsequent frightening journey through nothingness before he finally took shape again on his hill, had taken far more from him than she realised. She was driving him to find his limits, and he was a better man for it. The loss of self-control that he experienced with her was invigorating and he could hardly bear the thought of moving into the future without it.

Dougie gently shifted her body onto the bed of skins and turned on his side, laying one arm over her protectively. It was almost time, though he knew he would be spending the night thinking. There was no longer any real choice. His pathway lay clear before to him. Now it was only a question of working out the details.

1980

The room was too hot. The afternoon sun slanted in through the hole in the net curtains and steamed on the floorboards beside his bed. The blankets were too heavy, and the air felt as if there was no oxygen left in it. *Stifling. The perfect word.*

Aidan tossed and turned, pushing the bedclothes onto the floor and exposing his skinny legs and too-white torso. Even wearing just pants, it was too hot. He wished someone would come in and open the window for him.

As if drawn by his soundless call, the door opened and Emily came in. She was carrying a glass of water, which chinked with the magical sound of ice cubes. Aidan pulled himself into a sitting position as she placed the glass on his bedside table and helped him get comfortable against the pillows. She held the glass to his lips and he sipped slowly, revelling in the sensation of cool water slipping down his throat. As he swallowed he began to choke, and she hurriedly put down the glass while he coughed.

The effort left him white and shaking, and he slid back down onto the mattress, curling himself round the tremors that shook his slender frame. Emily was guilt stricken.

"I'm so sorry. I thought it would help. Are you all right?"

The most foolish of questions. He was not all right, and suspected he never would be again. Emily meant no harm, though. He knew she cared.

"I'm fine," he managed. "The water was lovely. Just what I wanted."

"It didn't seem that way." Confidence back, she stood with hands on her hips, glaring at him. "It seemed more as if I was killing you."

"Not you," he said, then wished he'd bitten the words back. Her eyes, stricken, stared at him from her shocked face. Aidan sighed. He knew the unspoken rules. You must never speak of dying, never so much as imply you have thought the word. You must protect others from the knowledge that you understand the true state of your illness. Most of the time he did well. It was only that sometimes, when he was at a low ebb, it would be a relief to be able to speak openly.

There was no-one he could talk to about it. Emily was his best friend and confidante, as well as his sister, but she wasn't strong enough to know what he knew. The doctor was no use, and talked over his head, as if Aidan was incapable of understanding even the simplest medical terms. As for his mother and father, Mama was still in denial, and his father was far more concerned about her emotional needs than those of his son. "Bear up, son," was the sum of his helpful advice. "This is hard on your mother."

Aidan fell back on fictional characters, with whom he identified much more readily than any of the real people in his life, but he'd yet to find a protagonist whose fight was the same as his. He would far rather face the Minotaur in the fullness of its strength than this invisible enemy that possessed his body and tormented him with weakness and pain.

The coughing fit passed and Aidan uncurled. He shifted on the bed, trying to find a bit of sheet that wasn't already superheated.

"Open the window, there's a love," he said.

"I'm not supposed to. Mama says there are germs."

"Mama is still living in the nineteenth century. What's hurting me isn't caused by anything that comes through windows on the breeze. It's as hot as Hades in here. Please open it."

"All right, then. But if she finds out I'll be in for it. You owe me one."

Emily cracked open the sash and pushed the lower

window. It slid upwards for about an inch before sticking in its frame. Through the gap a blessed stream of cool air flowed. Thank goodness for Scottish summers: no matter how hot the sun, there was always a cool breeze somewhere.

"Will you read to me, Sis?"

"I suppose so. What do you want?"

"Anything Middle Earth or Narnian. Or some Andrew Lang, if you like."

"You know Mama doesn't like me reading you those. She says they give you ideas."

"That's the point of books."

"Oh, you know what I mean. Ideas about magical places outside of the world. Places that children can go to. She says *The Last Battle* isn't about a magical landscape at all, it's really about…" Her voice trailed off and she flinched, unable to meet his gaze.

"Death." The pithy syllable sat on Aidan's tongue.

"Don't say it."

"I'm the only person in this house who can say it and mean it."

Emily ignored this declaration, which she took to be self-pity. "Choose something else. Something Mama won't mind. What about *Jonathan Livingstone Seagull*?" This was Emily's current favourite read. Luckily, Mama hadn't looked beyond the pretty pictures.

Aidan felt a distinct sense of kinship with the philosophical bird. He shifted uncomfortably and grumbled, "It would be nothing but Pollyanna if it was all up to Mama."

"Now you're being mean. She just wants you to have hope. Anyway…" Emily's eyes sparkled. "The doctor phoned. He's been in touch with the hospital. They think they have a suitable bone marrow donor. They're going to start the treatment as soon as they can."

She patted him reassuringly and slipped out of the room, taking the water glass with her. She stopped outside the door, though. Aidan could hear her breathing. Time continued its slow progress, moments dropping like honey in the hot, still air of the room. The breeze from the window had died.

He lay back and stared at the ceiling. So, it was to happen. This would take some thought. He wasn't at all sure he was strong enough for what was ahead, nor whether he truly believed it could do any good. Only one thing was certain: a return to hospital would mean more pain.

He failed to notice the creak of floorboards as Emily tiptoed away. He left his wasted body far behind him as his mind ranged into the vast regions that inhabited his head. He hardly needed anyone to read to him. Each of his imaginary worlds stood fully formed and ready to be explored. He knew every word of his favourite books by heart.

Some decisions could only be reached in a place far away from the real world, with all its needles and mattresses and cold, white rooms—and people who demanded so much from him. With an effort he closed his eyes and summoned up an alternative reality.

Pain faded, and a cool, green landscape opened up before him as he sank into sleep.

17
☽ DRY AS OLD BONES ☾

The pleasant days of June trickled slowly by. Sushila found herself spending fewer days with Dougie. She had come to respect his demand for space, and tried to fill her time with other interests, recognising that so long as she was a participant in the living world she needed to behave like part of it and interact with other living beings. She walked every day to the little house round the corner to feed Mittens and give her clean water. The little cat gradually became accustomed to her presence and allowed her fur to be stroked, purring quietly, but she never permitted herself to be handled. After a few more days the old man came home, but Sushila continued to visit and often stopped for a cup of tea or a 'wee dram' with him.

She went to lunch several times with the ladies, and one day invited them all back to the White House for coffee and cakes. She had cheated and bought cakes from the bakery in town, but the tea and coffee were made with the spring water and she didn't think it was her imagination that they were all fizzing with laughter and life by the end of the morning. Afterwards Mary took her dog round to visit her father and his pets, but Morgan stayed behind to help with the dishes. Sushila found it pleasant to work quietly alongside the woman, sharing the work without any compulsion to chat, but she flushed when Morgan finally spoke. She looked Sushila up and down, her keen glance missing nothing.

"You're looking much healthier than when you arrived," she remarked. "You've a much better colour on you and I think your cheeks have filled out."

"It must be all this healthy island air," said Sushila.

"If I didn't know better I'd say you'd found yourself a man," Morgan said, shrewdly. Sushila ducked her head and hurriedly grabbed another plate to wash. "Except that I know there aren't any. They say if you want a man on this island you have to catch him before he gets off the ferry."

They laughed together, and Mary put her head round the kitchen door. "Talking about me?" she enquired.

"As if we haven't got better things to talk about." Morgan was dismissive, but smiled at Mary. "Ready to go?"

Mary nodded and Morgan hung up her tea towel and took her leave.

The house seemed quiet and a little empty without the women's chatter and gossip, and Sushila missed them, although it was a relief to stop guarding her thoughts and holding her tongue. A part of her desperately wanted to share the reality of her new life, but it was too secret, too vulnerable to share with the ladies, no matter how nice they were. One word to them and it would be all over the island: Sushila Mackenzie's going crazy, she's got an imaginary man. At best they would not understand, and at worst the teasing could be malicious if they suspected she was pulling their legs. No, they were not the people to tell.

And, to be honest, who else was there? For all that she was making an effort to get out and speak to people, her days away from Dougie were just that: a period of marking time while she waited to be with him again. She didn't want to end her life, even if it meant being one with him forever. She'd already reached that realisation. It meant she was going to live on for a long time in this house, to all intents and purposes alone, and she'd better come up with some kind of plan for her time, or she'd drive herself mad with impatience and that would do neither of them any good.

That led her, by roundabout paths of internal conversation, to the reminder that she still hadn't done anything about Dad. Well, that was something she could fix.

She took off her apron and hung it up to dry, then walked swiftly up the hill to a point where she found a mobile phone signal. Checking through her emails she noted that the London flat had sold and the funds were in the hands of her solicitor, awaiting the final details of probate. She logged onto the net and began looking at airline flights from Glasgow. Within a matter of half an hour or so she'd managed to book flights and a connecting train that would see her in Sri Lanka by the end of the month. There were three days available in the country, and she arranged accommodation near to the stretch of coastline where she'd once lived with Alan and Priya.

Three days was longer than she wanted, but she hoped it would keep Dougie happy. He would be able to see that she was making an effort to move on with her life, and it was hardly long enough for him to get into any trouble while she was away. She snorted. All evidence to date suggested that he was a long streak of trouble looking for opportunities. That wasn't going to change any time soon.

One advantage of her travel plans was that she would still be here for the summer solstice, which this year more-or-less coincided with the full moon. Even with her limited experience, Sushila recognised that this would be another of the high holidays of nature's calendar. Surely it would be an energy peak for Dougie, and they ought to be able to have a few wonderful hours together before she travelled? In fact, she was relying on it to give her the strength to tear herself away.

The morning of the solstice dawned clear, cool and grey, with clouds covering the sun. Dougie had spent the night, though they'd done no more than talk about her travel plans. She sat on the edge of the bed, between his thighs, as he slowly brushed her hair; a poignant reminder of her second night in his house which left her speechless with pleasure. After that, sleep was restful and easy.

She moved dreamily about the kitchen, preparing

breakfast, and sighed as he came up behind her and dropped a kiss on the back of her neck. She leaned back against him and felt his morning erection against the small of her back. A wicked thought crossed her mind and she acted on it, drawing him down to the cold floor of the kitchen where she had once fantasised taking him, the day she first realised what he truly was. 'Water vampire' didn't frighten her any more, if indeed it ever had. It was simply part of him, and she wanted to love and accept every aspect of his strange second life.

After a few moments of fumbling and kisses she gave up. It wasn't what she wanted now, and anyway it was clear his interest had subsided. In fact, he seemed subdued and moved to stand at the kitchen workbench, staring out of the window across the yard to the base of his hill. She pressed a mug of tea into his hand and left him while she finalised her packing. She wasn't due to leave until the mid-afternoon ferry the following evening, but in the meantime needed to arrange return of the hire car and to check through her list of travel necessities. She wanted to be able to spend tonight on the hill without any trivial tasks left undone. Tonight was for the two of them alone, and the memory of it would have to carry her through their time apart.

She'd taken on board his comments about glamour, for all that she'd disagreed with them at the time. There was a pull between them, like the dark magic of gravity; it took an effort of will each time she walked away from him, and after the horrible moment where she'd lost him on the Ben she felt as though there was a thin but almost tangible cord connecting them. Wherever he was, she felt him, and she believed he responded to her in the same way. She wondered if that connection could survive travel away from the island. She feared not, and that meant the next few days would hold a world of loneliness for both of them. It wasn't going to be easy.

In the afternoon they climbed the hill hand in hand, pausing to drink at the spring. Then, the grass springy and soft under her feet, Sushila passed into the hidden valley and felt her spirits rise in its calm and welcoming embrace. They made love slowly and tenderly on a bed of new grass and wild flowers, a fairy's arbour of willow and hazel woven into a bower over their heads. It was obvious that Dougie had created this for her and she showed her delight by tumbling him on the soft turf and taking him with joyous laughter.

They lay for long hours in the leafy shade, touching one another, learning each other's ticklish spots and most responsive places, as the sun seemed to stand still in the sky. At last, as evening fell, they made their way to his house where food and drink were waiting for them.

Tonight there was no thunderstorm, no elemental display. Instead, a light rain fell all night, soaking the ground with its blessing, and Sushila felt herself borne away on the gentle current of his love for her. Slowly, and with consummate skill, he stripped away the layers of her clothing and touched her with his fingers, his tongue, all the strong, firm length of him that she'd come to know so well. She touched him too, relearning every part of him from the hair that she loved to run her fingers through to those oh-so-ticklish toes. She made him writhe as she stroked them. But it was clear that the evening was all about her needs, and he set about raising her to new heights of arousal.

Shaken and consumed by passion as wave after wave of pleasure coursed through her, she was aware that he was using every quantum of energy he could draw from her; but he gave it back in manifold ways, so that she was constantly subsumed in waves of delicious weakness alternating with surges of strength and vitality. Sleep came at a moment of ecstasy when, just as it had at the spring equinox, the sheer power of Dougie's presence overwhelmed her and she could take no more. Dimly, at the far edge of hearing, as her awareness slipped away she felt a sound, heard a movement, sensed on some subconscious level a change in the weather. But she was already far into sleep and it was only for a moment. With a sigh she relaxed in his arms and let go.

In the small hours of the night she came out of sleep to hear him moving around the room. When he crawled back into the bed his skin was cold, as if he'd been bathing in ice. She kissed his shoulder and tasted spring water on his skin. He gathered her in to himself, and she curled up inside the shelter of his body. For a moment she allowed herself to believe that this happiness could continue forever, but just thinking it was enough to invite dull reality back into the picture. Today she was going to have to leave this magical valley and go back to the real world. Only long enough to lay Dad to rest, she promised herself. Straight there and straight back. Dougie sighed and pulled her closer, and she gave herself back to peaceful sleep, content in the moment.

She woke to a shaft of sunlight in her eyes. She blinked, blinded for a moment, and rolled over in the bed. Her outstretched hand scuffed against rough grass and rock. She shot bolt upright and opened her eyes.

She was sitting, fully dressed and booted, on a patch of rough ground, dry and dusty with low grasses and outcrops of lichened rock. There was no sign of the house, the clearing or the stream. She looked about herself, wildly, feeling an intense sense of disorientation. In her ears she felt the last echoes of a sound too low-pitched for hearing, like the anguished groan of an earthquake deep in the rock. She jumped to her feet and shouted.

"No! No…"

Frantically she searched, desperate to find some recognisable landmark. She ran from one end of the dusty valley to the other and back, quartering the hillside, covering the same ground over and over. She told herself this was a practical joke. He'd lifted her in her sleep and placed her here. This wasn't his valley. She bent low over the turf, searching for any sign of moisture-loving plants, stopping from time to time and holding her breath, reaching with every pore of her being to hear over the pounding of her heart the faint trickle of water that would tell her where to find the spring. At last her feet scuffed on a smooth surface and she looked down, at a flagstone polished by generations of footsteps. Or centuries of weathering.

Lying beyond it was a jumble of stones, jutting out from the grass. She fell to her feet and patted the ground between them; felt, for a moment, a fading sense of warmth, as from embers of a fire that had died long ago. She lay at full length and pushed her face into the earth, smelling the faintest scent of ashes, almost at the edge of perception, the aroma disappearing as soon as she'd identified it. She rubbed the earth on her cheeks, but no particle of ash remained. The valley was as dry and sere as desert, and looked as though no human being had set foot in it for decades. And yet, here was Dougie's porch stone. She shook her head savagely, but couldn't shake the conviction. Here. She'd fallen asleep here, cradled in his embrace. She had woken here, in the same place. It couldn't be. It just couldn't be.

Still refusing to accept the evidence of her eyes, Sushila staggered up the small valley towards the summit of the hill. As she reached it she groaned and fell to her knees, hitting her forehead again and again on the unyielding ground. A cloud of yellow dust hung in the air, obscuring the terrible truth that was clamouring at her, insisting she recognise it. The hilltop had collapsed in on itself, leaving a rubble-filled hollow where the crest had been. The ground around it was parched. There was no spring here. There could never have been a spring in this dry place. Lying in the grass at the edge of the circle of devastation she found her small pack.

Numbly, Sushila stood and pulled it onto her shoulders. Moving wearily, as if in the grip of a terrible but compulsive dream, she scrambled around the edge of the collapse until she reached the south-east side of the hill. There, at the very edge of the rubble field, she found a small hollow, lined with stones and covered with a mesh to protect the pipe that jutted from it. The hollow was as dry as old bones. There was no sign that water had ever run there.

She fell to her knees again in front of the springhead,

wrapping her arms around herself and rocking backward and forward. The only sound she could make was a low moan, torn out of her by a refusal to believe what she saw. Tears welled in her eyes and dropped onto the dry stones, where they vanished as if they had never been. Summoning all the strength she possessed she willed the stream back into life, squeezing her eyelids together as she tried to force her dream into being. At last she opened her eyes again, the deep lines between them separating two blank orbs that stared, unseeing, at the dry ground in front of her.

Slowly, painfully, as if it hurt to move, she climbed to her feet. She opened her mouth as if to speak, but said only one word on a wave of terrible pain.

"Dougie."

There was no reply. Slowly, painfully, she made her way down to the White House at the foot of the hill, the house that was not, had never been her home. As she went the dry, sere voice of the wind murmured in the soft burr of a beloved voice; whispering in her ear, over and over, its wordless but unmistakable song.

"You need to live, Sushila Mackenzie. You have so much to live for."

And once, swimming up from her memory, repeating the words he'd said to her a lifetime ago, in the strength and joy of their first joining.

"Today I feel as though I could move mountains."

2015

It was dark and still in the cave. Minute drops of water coalesced from the rock face, infinitesimally slowly, and pooled at its base. The air was damp and cool and smelled of wet rock, and buried sunshine.

"Petrichor."

The old man grunted, and the woman shifted in the darkness, squatting over the fire pit. A brief flare lit the cave, sending shadows flickering, then subsided into a warm glow. She spoke again.

"Petrichor. It means the smell of earth after rain. The oils of plants, and soil dissolved in rainwater. It's our smell."

The old man muttered indistinctly and it was her turn to grunt. She rested a kettle on the embers and watched it, broodingly, as steam began to filter into the chamber. She sighed, and the old man shuffled forwards and laid his hand on her shoulder. She leaned against him, taking comfort from the touch.

"What about the boy?"

She sighed again. "Tantrums and foolishness. All that fuss over a mortal."

"He loves her."

"And what would you know about that." She shuffled round in the darkness and peered up into his face. "You never understood when I went back into the world. Why is this different?"

The man forbore to answer. She sniffed. "Men," she said. "Ten thousand years and it makes no odds. You're all strangers."

A rich, herbal smell filled the dank space and the old man took the bowl from her eagerly and sipped it, blowing on its surface to cool the tea. He squatted, half-hidden in the shadows, flickers of firelight glinting off the gannet, the orca, the salmon, the narwhal, coiling in blue patterns around his torso. "He grieves," he said. "When he wakes there will be pain."

She nodded, sipping her own tea as the fire slipped back into darkness. "Then we will let him sleep," she said. "And when he wakes he will turn to us."

The old man grunted again. It was not agreement. "There will be storm again on the hilltop before that day comes," he said.

18
☽ THE SEA GIVES ☾

The morning sun was still below the horizon when Ruwan noticed the slim figure of the woman making her way down to the water's edge. She walked all the way to the water and dipped her fingers into the waves, shifting whatever she was holding from one hand to the other as she washed each in turn. Once done she backed out of the water, paused for a moment with her gaze on the slowly lightening horizon, and turned to make her way back up the beach.

He stood, still as a statue in the shadows. He was pretty sure she hadn't noticed him, and he didn't want her to. This was a precious chance to admire and desire, without fear of discovery. He shuffled his bare feet in the sand and put one hand behind him, flat against the side of the hull. He'd been doing this job for weeks now, although today was the final test. He wasn't worried. He'd worked hard and planned meticulously; it was all going to go off without a hitch. This was the best opportunity he'd ever been offered and he still couldn't believe his luck.

The woman hitched up her sarong and squatted down to scoop out a shallow depression in the sand. She placed whatever she was holding carefully in the depression and pulled out a cigarette lighter. Ruwan could see the small flame clearly in the half-light. Suddenly it dawned on him that what she was doing was a private thing, not for his eyes. He turned away and gave his attention back to the boat. The hull was clean now, and in a few more minutes there'd be enough light for him to start work on the engine. He resigned himself to patience: the woman could wait. He'd be seeing her soon enough.

***

Sushila shifted her footing until she felt more stable, and carefully held the flame to the pile of wood shavings she'd created. The flame flickered and steadied as the wood caught. As the little fire grew she gradually added more pieces, until at last all that was left of the broken box was the lid. For a moment she held it close to her heart before placing it carefully on top of the pile. She watched the fire closely as the wood was consumed, darting in with a finger to quickly rearrange it when it seemed that one side was burning faster than the other.

At last it died down to a pile of soft ash. She pushed some sand over the top to cut off the oxygen and kill the fire, and stirred through the sand and ash mix to make sure that there was nothing left unconsumed. Once the mix had cooled a little, she gathered most of it into a fold of her sarong and carried it down to the water's edge.

This was the last move in a process that had taken several months in the making. At first, she'd been unable to do anything other than lie on the hilltop with her fists clenched in agony, refusing to believe what she knew to be true. The pain she felt was like nothing she'd experienced before. The final healing moment of her past grief, when she realised that she'd truly let Alan go and that she mourned him only as one should for an old friend long gone, was when the pain of losing Dougie tore her heart from her chest and left her with a gaping wound so immense that even breathing caused unbearable pain. She had tried to stop breathing; she had tried so hard. In those first moments, if she could have followed him she would have. Life was utterly empty without him.

She didn't doubt for a moment that he'd done it deliberately. All those conversations about how she would enjoy life back in Sri Lanka. All those arguments where she'd accused him of wanting to get rid of her. All those fears she'd had about how to create a life that could successfully juggle the years ahead in the living world with her entrance into the supernatural world of the spring. He'd seen it from the beginning: Mad Mrs Mackenzie, who was away up the hill half the time and claimed to see ghosts. There was no normal life for her if she stayed with him. When she refused to accept it, when she made it clear that she intended to stay with him no matter how difficult it was, he'd taken matters into his own hands.

It must have been two or three nights later that she half walked, half fell down the hill and into the porch of the White House, dehydrated and raving with sleeplessness and grief. In her struggle to get to the water in its container she'd spilt most of it over the kitchen floor. The food in the fridge had all gone off. How long had she been away? She found some stale bread and choked it down, scrabbling at the water puddle to get more to drink, and once she'd assuaged the worst of her thirst she sat with her back against the kitchen cabinets and howled a cry of terrible pain, because she knew she'd chosen to live.

After that it was just a process of planning things. First, planning to stand up and change her clothes; to wash herself and brush her hair; to trudge up the hill far enough to get a signal so that she could call Mary and ask for help. It was all she could do to put on a facade of normality when Mary arrived and took her into town to buy food and water. She doubted there would ever be a water supply for the house again. She couldn't bring herself to care.

Mary came back every day for a week. She was obviously concerned, but Sushila wouldn't talk about it. Even thinking about talking caused a blockage to form in her throat, cutting off her voice. She managed to talk about meaningless things: I need bottled water… I must buy some food… I will be going away soon… I need to find a caretaker for the house.

Slowly, painfully slowly, all the bits of planning fell into place and the time for leaving crept closer. Sushila tried to deny it, sitting hunched up in the bedroom with Dad's ashes in their box clutched in her lap, weeping the tears over them that she couldn't let fall for Dougie. But his sacrifice would have been meaningless unless she came to that one decision, and after she made it and booked new flights everything else seemed to fall into place. By mid-July she was ready to leave. No, not ready—she would never be ready—but there was nothing more to do. She was numb from carrying around the terrible, empty nothingness that consumed her. She had done what needed to be done, and now there was nothing. There would never be anything but nothing.

She climbed back up the hill several times, unable to let go the need to excoriate herself again and again with the pain of loss. Each time the same sight met her at the top of the hill: the summit fallen in on itself, the spring dry, the ground dusty and stony, almost nothing green at all left in the area of the collapse. There was not the slightest drop of moisture to be had anywhere, and the cord that once bound them so strongly had snapped back on itself, doing terrible damage as it did so.

It didn't seem right that she could walk around in the world and no-one could tell that she was hollow. But it was true. It was possible to live with emptiness. It was possible that no-one else could tell the difference. She'd done it after the tsunami. After a while she acknowledged a familiar feeling: her body possessed the habit of survival at times when everything seemed lost. It knew what to do, and she let it.

The flight was as meaningless as everything else, and when they landed she stood and waited numbly, case in hand, for the call to leave the plane. As she dragged her luggage down the corridor towards the arrivals lounge it occurred to her that only four months previously she would have been utterly unable to do such a thing. Briefly, the pain of that thought shocked her out of her stupor and she felt the full weight of her loss. It bent her in two, falling forward over a pain so intense she thought it would break her, but it passed and the numbness returned, all too soon.

It wasn't until she stood on the deck of the small boat, leaning over the side as the skipper held its bow into the wind, letting the handfuls of ash sift through her hand and drift away on the salt breeze, that tears came easily and freely into her eyes and she let them fall.

"Goodbye, Dad. You're with Mum now. There'll never be any more pain. You're free."

One by one the beloved faces passed before her eyes: the little grandmother who had raised her and cherished her; the beautiful mother whose attention she had always craved; the wonderful man who had made her a woman and who had intended to make her his wife; the loving father who had wanted the world for her, and gave her his creativity and his joy in life. And the man who had loved her, healed her and, in a very meaningful way, died for her: the man who held her soul in his keeping, wherever her heart might lead her.

And with that Sushila realised: she had her heart back. Broken and scarred, still it beat in her chest and it insisted on life. That was the gift Dougie had given her, and the only way to thank him would be to go forward and live.

***

She stood at the water's edge and brushed the remaining sand and ash from her fingers, letting go the last fragments of her father's life and picking up the threads of her own. Walking further up the beach she approached the white boat on its trestle, a pair of brown legs sticking out from underneath it. She paused to admire the length of them, and their well-muscled calves.

"Hi, Ruwan. How's she looking?"

Ruwan's legs disappeared and he slid out from the far

side of the hull and jumped to his feet.

"She's looking great."

He tried without success to wipe the grin from his face. He was perfectly aware that he wasn't talking about the boat, but he didn't mind if she misunderstood his meaning. Sushila smiled at his enthusiasm and Ruwan basked in what he had privately begun to call 'the smile of the most beautiful woman in Sri Lanka'.

Sushila ran her fingers along the transom. "Will she be ready in time?"

"She's ready now. I'm just checking things."

He nodded in satisfaction and ducked under the boat, coming up on the same side as Sushila. Her smile was even more gorgeous close up. He wiped his hands on a rag and offered one to her. She shook it solemnly; he couldn't help admiring her small hand with its slender fingers looking so vulnerable clasped in his own. He loved everything about her, from her slim hands to her beautiful hair, and even that slight hitch that she got in her stride when she was in a hurry. It wasn't really noticeable, not unless you were looking for it, though he always was. He'd lost heart and mind to this woman and he was determined to give her whatever she needed. He only hoped that she needed a lot.

"Our first paying clients today," she reminded him, as if he needed it. He'd personally booked every one of them, and knew their names, their ages and their family relationships. She gave him that lovely smile again as she continued, "Let's hope they enjoy themselves and tell their friends."

"Everybody loves whales. They're going to love it."

"That's if we can find any whales." Her words were sombre but their tone was not.

"We'll find them." In her presence he was utterly confident.

He glanced across and saw her eyes sparkling in the newly risen sunlight. He couldn't help but believe those eyes were sparkling for him, and he intended to do everything in his power to make sure that she kept on shining.

2019

Dee hung upside-down from the barbed wire fence. It had seemed like a great adventure that morning, setting out to climb the hill with a packed lunch and some midge repellent in her bag. The day dawned bright and clear, with barely a threat of cloud in the west, so she told her mother she was off to explore.

"Take care," her mother said. "Be back by six."

She'd failed on both counts.

It was fine to begin with. She strode up the hillside with a fine air of bravado, putting as much distance between her and the house as possible. Far behind her she heard a yell. It sounded like her name, floating on the breeze, but she pretended she hadn't heard it. Her breath began to come fast and she felt the blood thudding in her ears, but she pushed on all the way to the upper fence line.

This time when she looked back she could see two small figures standing by the back door. Good. Dad had finally got up. Well, it served him right if he'd planned an outing. He should have got up earlier. She stopped herself, cutting off the flow of mental grumbling. *This is my holiday, too. I deserve to do what I want.*

One of the figures was waving a white cloth at her: Mum, with a pillowcase off the washing line. Dee waved back and turned away.

She wandered all morning, criss-crossing the hills, once taking off her boots to slog through a stream, slipping on the wet rocks, wincing at the feeling of hard stone on her city-soft feet. She ate her lunch with her back against a boulder, gazing across the blue valley to distant peaks, no doubt dotted by the same half-wild sheep that flitted away whenever she came near them.

There hadn't been a soul around all day, but she'd been delighted by the lilting cry of a skylark, soaring into the blue; by the comfortable maa-ing of fat sheep, ready for shearing by the looks of them; by the little flowers that fought for a place in the well-grazed turf. In a sunny patch by a rock she found a clump of pink spotted orchids which had somehow escaped the hungry mouths of the sheep. It was a perfect day.

She'd been overconfident. Somewhere, she'd taken a wrong turn. While she was eating lunch a mist came down, and the glorious view faded to a circle a few yards across, with herself in the centre. She tried to work out which way to walk, to head home, but lost all sense of direction in the mist. She found herself sliding down a long scree slope, which seemed to offer a quick way down the hillside but proved dangerously unstable. She began to think she heard noises: voices in the mist, vague shapes moving just outside the circle of her vision. She thought about being a stranger here. Perhaps the mountain didn't want her walking on its slopes. The feeling of presence in the mist grew stronger, and she began to run.

All of a sudden the mist lifted and she found herself at the base of the scree slope, running straight into a ragged, half-broken fence wound around with coils of barbed wire. Too close to stop, she cannoned into the mass and jumped right over it. She thought she'd cleared it, but a finger of wire caught in her trousers and gripped her, the force of her leap flipping her upside down. She struggled to right herself, but the barbs caught on her hair and clothing, so that the more she struggled, the more tightly caught she became.

That was hours ago. It was hard to tell in the Scottish summer—it never really got dark—but she had a feeling it was at least ten o'clock. Hours after she was supposed to be home. Of course they would look for her, but she had no idea where she was. It could be hours. It could be days. If they found her at all. She stifled a sob at the thought. She cried at first, when her struggles failed to free her, but the tears ran into the corners of her eyes and her nose blocked up, being upside-down. For a moment she felt she couldn't breathe, until she took control and forced the tears down again. She told herself not to panic. It was just a question of enduring until she could be rescued. Now, to make matters worse, it was raining.

Dee turned her head on one side, as best she could with the barbs caught in her hair. It was enough to get the worst of the rain out of her eyes. Her sodden fringe dripped onto the stones beneath her head. She was soaked to the skin and beginning to feel the chill. If it rained all night like this, she might not last long enough to be found. Really scared now, Dee cried out then bit down on it. She'd called and called. No-one was near enough to hear her, and her throat was already hoarse from yelling. She needed to save her voice, in case someone passed by.

Shivering, she closed her eyes against the half-light of summer midnight and tried to keep calm. She shook with cold, and her head began to swim. It couldn't be good to hang like this; heads weren't meant to be lower than feet for hours on end. Still shivering, she escaped into an uneasy sleep.

A low, murmuring voice came out of the darkness up on the hill. Dee came slowly awake, realising that she'd been hearing it for some time: an old voice, singing in a language that she couldn't understand. By its cadence, the song seemed to be a lullaby. Dee could hear the rain, pattering on the ground, and the stream rushing away down the hill, but no water was falling on her. She still hung pinioned on the fence, but the air around her was warm and faintly scented, and her clothes were dry.

Well, that didn't make sense. With a feeling of relief, Dee realised she was dreaming and let herself drift away again on the current of the strange song.

She jerked awake, the sun in her eyes as it rose out of a thick bank of mist on the valley floor. Voices. She heard voices, and one of them was calling her name. She swallowed a lump in her throat and croaked out a call, then louder as the voices came nearer.

"Dee. Oh, thank goodness." It was Dad. He filled her field of vision, along with the booted feet and corduroy clad legs of one of their neighbours.

"Lie easy now," the man said. "We'll soon have you out of there." He pulled a pair of snips out of his trouser pocket and began to cut the wire.

"Why on earth did you have those with you?" Dad asked.

"Who cares!" shouted Dee, but silently, inside her own head. She was just happy she'd been rescued.

"Oh, well," the man said. "You often find an old ewe caught up in one of these bits of fence. Best to get 'em off before they starve."

19
☽ THE WIND ON THE HILL ☾

The white people carrier pulled into the small dusty farmyard and an explosion of children happened. There were adults among them, and some began to empty the vehicle of luggage, while others went to open up the house and prepare it to receive visitors. For a brief period no-one remembered the old lady in the front passenger seat, but at the door one boy turned and looked back.

"Hurry up, Grandma." He stood with hands on hips and regarded her. "I'll give you a hand," he announced, but he'd hardly begun to skip back when one of the men walked round from the back of the vehicle and opened the passenger side door.

"Here you go, Mum."

The old woman gingerly edged down from the high seat, gripping her son's arm firmly until she was securely on the ground. She wore a knee-length house coat and flat sandals. Beneath her skirt her legs were skin and bone, not an ounce of fat but still ropy with muscle. She freed herself from his grip and adjusted the tube in her nose. Carefully, he handed down the heavy oxygen cylinder in its trolley and she took hold of it with one hand, leaning on its familiar weight, while the other grasped a walking stick. Slowly she made her way towards the front door of the house; too slowly for the boy, who tired of holding the door open and disappeared inside. The door closed with a bang just as the man shouted.

"Danny…? Oh, I don't know why I bother." Muttering, he put his head back into the rear of the vehicle and more suitcases and bags came flying out.

The old woman ignored him and continued her shuffling walk. Halfway across the yard she paused and leaned on her stick, puffing steadily as she forced air into her damaged lungs. She raised her head and gazed up the slope of the hill beyond the fence. It rose, green and brown, into the blue heavens, and far up its slopes she could hear the skylark singing. Purple patches of early heather coated its flanks and an impressive thunderhead of cloud raised itself behind the summit. Despite the mostly clear sky, there was a smell of rain in the air. A smile of pure joy crossed her face and she grasped the stick more securely and began her walk again.

The door banged open and the boy was back. "Aren't you there yet?" he demanded.

"Always in a hurry, you are." She grimaced at him, though he was quick to sense the smile beneath the pretended scowl. "Always in such a hurry. I don't know how you manage to stay as fat as you are, the way you run around so much."

The boy gasped in mock outrage. "I'm not fat. Anyway, Mum says I'm due for a growth spurt."

She lifted her cane and poked him in the stomach with it. "Looks like fat to me." She cackled in a menacing but ultimately affectionate way, channelling her inner witch the way that only very old women can do.

The boy ducked back into the house again and the door banged shut, but it was opened immediately by an older girl. She looked the woman over with a worried expression and came into the yard to offer her arm in support. "Come on, Grandma. Let's get you inside. There's a nice chair that's perfect for you."

"I know that chair, you hussy. Don't try to tell me what's in my own house. Just because you've come here for holidays, and I haven't, doesn't mean I don't know my own possessions."

By this time they'd reached the house and the small, tired footsteps continued through the porch and on into the living room. There a familiar chair was waiting, and the girl settled her into it. "Can I get you anything, Grandma?"

"I'd like a cup of tea. None of your mother's herbal stuff either. Proper tea." She suffered the girl to fuss around her with cushions and a footstool, but only for a moment. She poked her experimentally and the girl yelped.

"Sorry."

She didn't sound as if she meant it, and the girl rolled her eyes in a long-suffering way.

A woman put her head round the door. "What are you doing to Milly? If you're unkind to them it'll be no surprise if they stop helping you, Mum."

The woman snorted contemptuously, but looked at Milly out of the corner of her eye. Milly grinned at her and pranced off.

"Now, we're going to leave the unpacking until later this evening. The kids are ravenous. We're going into town to get fish and chips. Do you want to come with us?"

"When I've only just got settled? No. I want a nice cup of tea and then some peace and quiet. So you can all go away."

"All right, then. You can have your peace and quiet, and we'll take them away and let them have a run on the waterfront. We won't be long. I think we'd better see about getting you into bed once we're back. You look tired."

She walked away, calling the children to her, and Sushila scowled at her retreating backside.

"I am tired," she mumbled to herself. "Too bloody tired. But not for much longer." The thought cheered her and she awarded herself a private grin. It was irritating being so dependent on other people. Just as well things were almost finished. "Too much bloody fuss." She shifted uneasily in the chair, but roused herself to smile cheerfully at Milly, whose worried face had popped round the side of the door. Her mother looked in over her shoulder.

"Are you sure you're going to be all right, Mum?" She came across the room and adjusted Sushila's pillows before kissing her gently on the cheek.

"I'll be fine. Peace and quiet, just what I need." She patted the woman on the arm. "You've always been a good girl, Aby."

"Well, make the most of it. We'll not be long."

Within minutes the family had tumbled back into the vehicle and driven away. The change in the old house's atmosphere was almost palpable, as serenity washed back in with the light breeze through the window. Sushila sat in her dad's old armchair with her feet on the footstool, oxygen cylinder to one side and a handy table to the other, holding a steaming mug of proper Scottish tea made with proper Scottish milk. She eyed it with satisfaction, but relaxed back in her chair without drinking any.

It had been a long day. They'd arrived on the midday ferry, but the weather was so lovely that they'd driven round the island the long way and spent the afternoon at the famous white sand beach. Half the population of the island seemed to have been there, making the most of the first hot summer day, and the kids had enjoyed themselves ducking in and out of the water and making sandcastles. She remembered other picnics at other beaches, in other parts of the world. Her children had been so much fun. But they grow up and leave and have children of their own, and all of a sudden you're old and tired and it's all too much. She loved them all. She always would. But a long life well lived had worn her out and she was quietly glad that it had almost come to an end.

Sushila sat and soaked up the peace. Inside the house there was nothing to hear but the faint and irregular pattern of her heartbeat and an occasional hiss when she drew on the oxygen. She closed her eyes to look once again on the beauty of the island's coast and its cerulean sea, and the ghost of a beautiful smile flickered across her lips.

"We never did find out whether you could go to the sea," she murmured.

As she sat back in the familiar chair in the once so

familiar room, one that she hadn't entered for over fifty years, her mind slipped back easily into the past. She could feel again, gossamer thin, the memory of a thread that had once been a binding as strong as steel cable. She sighed and relaxed, all of a sudden feeling safe and secure.

At last, she was back in the place she had longed for. At last, she was allowed to rest. Her breathing slowed as she slipped into sleep: slowed, slowed… her tired heart reaching for the peace that she hoped to find. Slowly. In perfect faith. Until peace claimed her, between one breath and the next, as sweetly as his loving had claimed her all those years ago.

And up on the hill where moisture welled slowly between two mossy stones, bordered forever with late spring flowers, a little breeze arose and set the grasses dancing.

> Carry me down and lay me
> Where you will.
> My heart will lie quiet,
> Wherever you put me,
> And I'll not stir.
>
> I will turn away,
> Into stillness of air:
> Drowsy days,
> An endless season of peace.
>
> There'll be no more tears.
> The words and the fire
> Will go to earth
> And rest serene.
>
> In dappled days and dark,
> In the corner of the picture,
> At the limit of your vision:
> You'll not find me where you look.

But I will still be here,
In the wind on the hill.

☽ THE END ☾

TIMELINE

Dates in italics appear as histories in the book. The rest are implied, or mentioned in Dougie and Sushila's conversations.

9400BCE	*Drowning boy.* The blue man of later histories.
783AD	*Pregnant woman escaping Vikings.* Her baby becomes the *caileach*/matriarch of Dougie's family.
1774	*The blue man and the woman atop their hill.* She is about to enter the human world.
1793	*Old woman collecting wool for the wise woman.*
1794	*Birth of a baby.* Dougie's great grandfather.
1802	*Clearance of the village on the hill.* The *caileach* and her son.
1891	Donald born.
1894	Dougie born.
1897	*Woman and child.* Dougie and his mother, who dies shortly afterwards.
1901	*Man, boy and sheep.* Dougie and his father.
1902	Dougie and Donald's father goes away (Boer War).
1904	*Dougie and the leaking roof.*
1906	*Dougie and Maire at school.*
1909	*Hunting the stag.* Donald 18, Dougie 15.
1914	*Donald goes away. Dougie gets the tattoo.*
1915	Eilidh MacDonald has a baby boy (Archie).
1915	Gran/*caileach* 'dies'.
1915	Dougie marries Maire.
1916	Maire and the baby die.

1945	Eilidh MacDonald's son dies.
1953	*Dougie dies.*
1955	*Donald comes home.*
1968	Donald dies.
1973	*Dougie lives again.*
1980	*Aidan.*
2004	The Boxing Day tsunami in the Indian Ocean.
2014	*Sushila.*
2015	*Grandfather and Grandmother in conversation.*
2019	*Dee.*

GLOSSARY

Dougie MacLean is a Gaelic speaker, and even in English his conversation is peppered with Gaelic words. You can get a flavour of them from the list below. Please refer to any good dictionary for guidance on the pronunciation of Gaelic words.

Gaelic words and phrases:

Àlainn	Beautiful
Airgid	Silver (*Airgiduine* = silver man)
Balaich/a bhalaich	Boy
Bobain/a bhobain	Affectionate term for a boy
Cailleach	Old woman
Caraid/a charaid	Friend
Duine	Man
Each-Uisge	Water-horse/Kelpie. A malevolent entity
Feumaidh thu falbh	You must go
Gaol/a ghaoil	Love
Gillean/a ghillean	Boy or son
Glé mhath	Very good
Gowan	Blacksmith
Gràdh/mo ghràidh	(My) love
M'eudail	My treasure
Mo chridhe	My heart
Mo leannan	My beloved
Mór	Big
Nighean	Girl
Òg	Young
Piseag	Kitten
Slàinte mhath	Good health
Trobhad an seo	Come here

Scots words:

Blackhouse	*Traditional Hebridean house with no chimney*
Dominie	*A schoolmaster*
Fank	*An enclosure for livestock*
Gralloching	*Removing the entrails of a deer*
Haar	*A thick sea mist*
Lazybeds	*Raised beds fertilized with seaweed*
Piece	*An item of portable food such as a bannock or sandwich, or more commonly, long ago, a lump of congealed oat porridge*
Plaid	*A chequered or tartan woollen cloth*
Skelp	*To hit, frequently an older person smacking a child in pretended anger*

ABOUT THE AUTHOR

Yvonne Marjot was born in England, grew up in New Zealand, and now lives on an island in western Scotland. She has been making up stories and poems for as long as she can remember, and once won a case of port in a poetry competition (New Zealand Listener, May 1996). Her first volume of poetry, *The Knitted Curiosity Cabinet*, won the Brit Writers Award for poetry in 2012. Her novels *Walking on Wild Air* and the *Calgary Chessman* trilogy are published with Ocelot Press, and her book of short stories, *Treacle and Other Twisted Tales*, by Crooked Cat Publishing.

She has worked in schools, libraries and university labs, has been a pre-school crèche worker and a farm labourer, cleaned penthouse apartments and been employed as amanuensis to an eminent botanist. She currently has a day job (running the local public library) and three grown-up children, and would continue to write even if no-one read her work, because it's the only thing that keeps her sane. In her spare time she climbs hills, looks for rare moths and promises herself to do more in the garden.

ALSO BY YVONNE MARJOT

The Calgary Chessman
On a windswept beach on the Isle of Mull, Cas Longmore is walking away loneliness when she unearths a mystery in the sand. To Cas, torn between Scotland and her New Zealand home, the object seems as odd and out-of-place as herself.

The Book of Lismore
Cas and son Sam are confronted by the ghosts of the past on the island of Lismore. The mystery they uncover proves easier to solve than the ongoing conflicts in their personal lives, as each is faced with a fresh challenge.

The Ashentilly Letters
Cas is called home to New Zealand, where she is unexpectedly faced with an old acquaintance. Meanwhile, Sam and Niall manage to rewrite the history of the Roman Empire in Scotland with Sam's first university dig.

Treacle and Other Twisted Tales
The world is broken. We mend it with stories, and sometimes we need to tell the tale slant. Open this book and let yourself be swept away to strange lands, and familiar places made new. For there is magic in everything.

THE CALGARY CHESSMAN

The darkness was absolute. Crouched on the top step, I clung to the smooth surface of the door. I feared falling: the basement stairwell yawned below me and without visual cues it was hard to balance. My hands on the door were the only reliable guide to my surroundings while my eyes persisted in trying to see something—anything. Closing them summoned up flashes of red and green, but when I opened them and peered into the darkness, I saw nothing at all. My ears strained constantly for his footsteps, coming back to complete the process of my humiliation. But mostly I feared that he might not come back.

  I swallowed down the rising dread that I might miss my boy's departure on his first day of school. Better not to think of that: allowing worst case scenarios into my head only made them more likely. He couldn't leave me here all night. Could he? I shifted a little on my uncomfortable perch, but a twinge of pain from my arm reminded me not to move. I closed my eyes again and willed myself to calm. Slowly the fear filled darkness receded as I thought my way into a more pleasant memory.

  I took myself far away, to a hot, yellow New Zealand beach where a small, sturdy boy clad in nothing but a sunhat carried buckets of water to fill the moat of the castle we had just finished. I watched him as I decorated the towers with shells, stones and drapes of wet seaweed. Something that had started as a simple mound with a bucket-castle on top had spread to cover a vast area of ditches and piles, patted and shaped into turrets and bridges, tunnels and walls.

  The little figure poured and trudged, filled and

poured relentlessly, but still the water drained away before he could return with the next bucket load. I knelt down beside him and wiped away the grubby tear streaks. Then I set to work digging a trench, from the main moat towards the sea's edge. The task was hopeless: the receding tide gradually exposed more of the beach, and the sea slid further away. Sam gave in and passed his bucket to me, and hand-in-hand we wandered back to the picnic.

A few sandy sandwiches and a lukewarm drink later, Sam was successfully distracted: off this time in his shorts and beach shoes to investigate the rock pools. Considering the tears, I was reluctant to take him back when at last the tide began to turn. Sam insisted, though, and we climbed down the hill again at twilight, round the back of the farmhouse, skirting the old slip where bare rock was beginning to gleam in the growing dark. Down past the waterfall, with a final jump into my arms onto the beach, to watch the march of the tide against our battlements.

Sam was pleased to see the ocean finally rush up the trench and fill the moat but, to my amazement, he laughed with delight as the foamy wavelets, raised a little against an offshore breeze, made short work of his towers and walls. In a few moments, the whole construction had collapsed into a soggy pile, soon to be as flat as the beach around it.

I sighed, remembering other days when Sam and I had spent hours in the little cove, building and discovering: things about the world, and about each other. It sometimes seems as though all the other days of my life have been grey shadows, and only those golden Huna Cove days were truly lived. Almost all of my strong memories of Sam are focused there. Except for his birth, of course. I winced, and turned away from that. There are parts of my life I prefer not to think about. Embarrassing moments at school. Most of my marriage. And the events that began Sam's life, and changed mine forever.

My concentration wavered, and I opened my eyes again to darkness. I expected to feel the basement stairs and the enveloping dark, drawing me back into my nightmare, but something else was wrong. The ground beneath my body was bumpy and irregular, and my hand pressed against a rough, stone surface, not wood. I yelped as a cold sensation washed across my feet. That was water! I struggled to sit up, to draw my feet away, but I felt a rush of liquid soak my legs again as a terrible surge of pain swept upwards from my arm and across my chest. The red wave of agony washed across my mind and pulled me down into the darkness once more.